THE FINAL RETREAT

A NOVEL

STEPHEN HOUGH

The Final Retreat

A novel

SYLPH
EDITIONS

For Colin (1926–1982)
a different kind of father

𝔐ANCHESTER 𝔗ELEGRAPH

17TH DECEMBER 2010

The body of 29-year-old Fr Chiwetel Okafor was discovered yesterday morning hanging from an electrical wire in his bedroom. A note in his handwriting was found and it is presumed that he committed suicide. There is no suspicion of foul play.

Born in Lagos, Nigeria, he had been a supply priest for the Roman Catholic diocese of Altrincham since August 2008. He is survived by his parents and two younger sisters.

I had to do this. I'm so sorry for everything. Please forgive me. God forgive me.

Chiwetel

FROM: Rev. Luke Tremont
TO: Bishop Bernard Smith
SUBJECT:
DATE: 28 October 2010   2:17 PM

FEAST OF SS SIMON AND JUDE

Your Grace,

I had a phone call earlier today from Fr Joseph Flynn of Sacred Heart Church, Sale. He asked to see you on a matter of extreme urgency. You have a cancellation on Monday at 4 PM so I've taken the liberty of giving him that appointment.

In Jesus, Mary and Joseph,

Fr Luke
Secretary to the Bishop of Altrincham

SOLEMNITY OF ALL SAINTS

Dear Fr Joseph,

Thank you for visiting me this afternoon and for explaining your situation. As I said then, you now have to put your life completely into the hands of God, trusting Him to guide you along what seems like an impossible path.

I have spoken to Craigbourne and they can indeed find a place for you on their eight-day silent retreat beginning on the 8th, a week from today. I'm very pleased that you've agreed to do this at such short notice because I think it will help you to focus on the things that matter and to see more clearly what the next steps should be. An Individually Guided Retreat is a very free affair. Your spiritual director will visit you each morning and suggest points for reflection and meditation that day, and after that you're on your own. You should spend the day in silence, allowing the Holy Spirit to speak to you. Don't read too much but do go for some nice long walks in Craigbourne's lovely grounds. Let the emptiness fill you and cleanse you. God is there.

One thing I would encourage you to do whilst you're there is to keep a notebook, jotting down thoughts as they come to you. This can be a good way to focus your mind on how your relationship with God has changed over the years. Treat it almost like an autobiography. Go deep into the beginnings of your vocation, what made you want to follow the call to the priesthood in the first place, and what keeps you a priest now.

God is closer to us than we are to ourselves. He is on your side – and so am I. Whatever happens with this blackmail business I am here to support you in prayer and with my friendship.

In Christ,

+Bernard

THE NOTEBOOKS

God, I'm dreading this week.

I drove here yesterday in the rain, south on the motorway then finally turning off into one of Cheshire's dripping village lanes. The loneliness of a priest is not only experienced when he's at home, when his rooms creak in familiar silence, when lack of companionship reduces him to an eccentric conversation with himself; no, on drives like this, past houses aglow with families, blazing hearths on early evenings, banter and argument within, toys tripped over on worn rugs, cogs in domestic wheels turning with ease behind the semi-privacy of partly-drawn curtains – this is when the ache gnaws.

After a few miles, through the mist of condensation and the squeaking see-saw of the windscreen wipers, I saw the signpost for Craigbourne and turned sharp right into the long, tree-lined driveway. The path was pitted and puddled and the grounds unkempt, not in the way an old tweed suit has settled into confident shabbiness but with a weariness of spirit. This was a property where the gardener was out of his depth, had bitten off more than he could chew, had given up in exhaustion and handed the keys back to Nature in defeat.

As I drove up to the front it was almost dark except for some lights coming from the windows of the chapel on the left wing of the house. I was late. I found a parking space round the side, took my bags out of the boot, then walked back quickly in the rain to the main door, pushing it open with a sodden shoe. We were all meant to have arrived in the early afternoon for a brief conference with the spiritual director and then to have begun the retreat proper with Vespers. But Vespers was obviously now well underway, judging by the sound of singing as I stepped inside the entrance hall. I lingered for a moment, listening to the out-of-tune voices in the distance. It seemed as if they were coming from a foreign land and that I was an alien landed on its shore. I longed just to go to my room and lie down but I didn't know where to go or to which room I had been assigned, so I put down my bags next to a carved oak ottoman and walked reluctantly in the direction of the music.

I don't want to be here. I almost cancelled at the last moment but I know I have to go through with it. My bishop wants me here and I need to have him on my side. I've no idea how I can continue as a priest and if I don't leave the priesthood of my own volition I may end up being defrocked anyway, sent to a monastery somewhere to live a life of penance and reform.

'I rejoiced when I heard them say: Let us go to the house of the Lord.' I sat down at the back and looked around the badly-lit chapel as the psalm was being chanted. It was an ugly, dreary space, small for a church but spacious considering that it had originally been a ballroom in a private residence. Craigbourne began its life as a grand country house, abandoned after the Second World War when servants were scarce but it was impossible to get along without them. It opened as a retreat centre in the early 1970s and was now something of a tribute to that era – the boxy furnishings in the sanctuary, a garish orange rug under the wooden altar which in turn was draped with a cream polyester cloth stencilled with the crude image of a dove and the word 'PEACE' in floaty, grey lettering. There were also a few signs of a later conservatism. A lurid reproduction of the Polish Sister Faustina's Divine Mercy image hung in a cheap gilt frame, the red stream from the heart of Christ almost fluorescent in its vivid downward flow. And next to it was her champion: John Paul II as a vigorous, newly-elected Pope, his handsome Slavic features now all faded in the pitted, bubbled photo.

There was something really depressing about this room, once all a-rustle with silk and satin but now housing the tat of cheap statues and power-saving bulbs hanging from vulgar chandeliers. Catholics have terrible taste. They talk about the glories of Michelangelo and Palestrina and Dante but true Catholic style is nylon doilies and plastic rosaries and flickering electric candles. And don't let them reply that in this very simplicity flourish the pious sentiments of the poor and the uneducated, and that amongst all of this is true sanctity. Amongst all of this is true superstition. Plain and simple. Bad taste and bad theology. But who am I to talk? A plastic priest, a nylon hypocrite.

There were no breviaries in the pew where I was sitting so I couldn't join in. Instead I just sat there in the shadows, thinking, musing, dozing. How often have my closed eyes been a snooze rather than a prayer.

Vespers ended and we all stood up to leave. Hello John, hello Bill, hello Frank. Priests' fraternity. Thick as thieves. We moved to the dining room where soon the conversation petered out. We'd temporarily forgotten that we were meant to be silent on this retreat. Tongues reduced to murmuring then to silence as we took our seats. Bowls of thin soup arrived, too hot to taste, and white, gluey bread rolls. Cheap red wine from a screw-top bottle was poured into thick glass tumblers. It was now completely dark outside and still raining.

2   CRAIGBOURNE

Craigbourne was built by the wealthy Manchester merchant Sir Roger Castleton and donated by his grandson to the diocese of Altrincham in the 1960s. The cotton mills of Lancashire had paid for its bricks, and the strident screams of the shuttles which had shunted so efficiently and lucratively for Sir Roger were a chilling contrast to this building's majestic, tranquil repose on the outermost skirts of one of Cheshire's quainter parishes. The factories' stone floors thick with dust and spittle. Threadbare clothes on broken backs. Weary faces lined with grime. Filthy ears shot to deafness. Sweat. Stress. Short, cramped lives. And yet here, a few safe, oblivious miles away, Craigbourne's mahogany banisters, resting atop a line of portly, gouty spindles, curled up like two thick eyebrows from the wide entrance hall to the airy bedrooms above, their polished wooden floors cushioned with Persian rugs under soft-sinking feather beds. 'Remember man that thou art dust and unto dust thou shalt return.' Every day was Lent at the mill; no day passed at Craigbourne in those high-noon years without a five-course dinner.

I suppose in its time, the late Victorian apex of expansion ('wider still and wider', whether girth, dado or Empire), it had had a certain eccentric style. But it needed the bustle of servants and the commanding presence of the patriarch, with his mutton-chop whiskers and his drooping gold watch-chain, to reach its true theatrical potential. Since its acquisition by the diocese of Altrincham Craigbourne has combined the look of an Ikea showroom – badly assembled flatpack furniture with fake brass handles slightly askew and often loose – with the ugliest leftovers from an antique shop's clearance sale. Every room here contains a mishmash of styles, all of them hideous: lamps which shed no light and are chipped at the base; thin, too-short curtains which don't quite meet in the middle; sagging, foam-filled sofas; a teak Welmar upright piano; a nest or two of formica coffee tables. And mirrors. So many mirrors at Craigbourne. In every room large carbuncular frames sprayed with thick gold paint surround modern, Windex-clear glass, reflective eyes amplifying the ghastliness within, every piece of doss-house furniture appearing twice, with a scowl.

The bedrooms today – there are about twenty-five in plaster-board divisions carved out of the original layout – are at least clean and simple. One narrow, single (of course) bed; a bedside table with a light and (of course) a Bible; a rickety wardrobe on the opposite wall next to a sink with just enough space on its rim for a credit-card-size cake of soap; there too a plastic beaker, for drinking, toothbrush or perhaps even teeth; and finally a desk near the window at which I'm writing these notes. No personal computers are allowed but this is a good idea on a silent retreat when days are meant to be spent in meditation. Even a sleeping hard-drive, needing only the twitch of a mouse to awaken it to a billion windows, would be death to contemplation.

It's been raining pretty much constantly since I arrived yesterday so I've decided just to stay in my room and fill these pages – I brought a stack of notebooks along with me. At home, except for the odd poem jotted down on the back of a parish newsletter, I usually write at the computer. But typing makes me stiff and conventional and I'm finding here that handwriting is liberating. The flow on the page becomes the flow of memory and ideas – yes, it's that way round, craft before art. Not dissimilar to the spiritual life itself: start to act out your faith and you will strengthen your faith ... until, like me, you lose your faith.

3   FATHER NEVILLE

So every morning at 9:30 sharp (how terribly sharp) a firm knock at the door of my room. Not a knock when flesh muffles the impact, but a knock with the bone of the joint, aimed as carefully as a cue against a billiard ball. A man wearing an immaculate cassock walks in.

Father Neville is remarkably thin. Utterly sexless. Scrubbed to the bone. Shaved to the skin. Short hair parted with razor-blade precision, a clean pink line from forehead to crown. He sits down in a hard chair after entering my room, never leaning back (small mortifications are the best kind) but with his spine as rigid and unyielding as the back of the chair in which he sits. Always a smile, but from teeth not eyes. Utterly joyless but with a kind of earnest energy, a slap on the back for one who actually needs an arm for support. He has an unspoken impatience at my torpor – I can see it in the jerk of his neck, as if he wanted to throttle me to sanctity.

I must confess I took an instant dislike to him, my shepherd guide for those twenty tight-lipped minutes a day. Real saints are unaware that they are saints but Father Neville is a spiritual stockbroker carefully analyzing his investments: hours of prayer, visits to the Blessed Sacrament, Novenas, the Corporal Works of Mercy, the Spiritual Works of Mercy – all sturdy rungs on the ladder to holiness. And mortifications . . . oh, they deserve a new paragraph.

Sitting straight in the chair is only the beginning. Sleeping on the floor, taking cold showers, food deprivation. I watched him at mealtimes taking the smallest portions. As if an invalid he would nibble on scraps held on the narrow prongs of his fork, or take a mere graze of sponge and custard to his mouth. Always butterless bread, always milkless tea. And always under his cassock next to his skinny ribcage (how uncurious sexually I was) there was the hair-shirt. I know about this because he told me: 'A shortcut to intimacy with God, Father. Focuses the soul on prayer. All priests should wear one for at least an hour a day.' I'm sure he never took his off. And then, alongside all of this, the scourge. The knotted cords lashed against the body to destroy the heat of the flesh through the heat of the flaying. 'This must only be done under guidance from a spiritual director, Father,' he said to me, hinting that the slouching, soporific priest sitting before him was not ready for such heroism. I shudder as I imagine the railroad gashes under his cassock, his own spiritual director urging him on to ever greater levels of pain and sacrifice 'in imitation of our Lord and for the benefit of souls.' I wince at the thought of the encrusted red welts weeping, waiting to be awakened into further flow.

I don't know how much he knows about me from my bishop (probably the minimum, 'a priest facing challenges in his spiritual life' perhaps, or 'issues with the sixth commandment') but it is clear that Father Neville has already snuffed out illicit passion in his own life with great success, as if kneeling next to a bathtub squashing flat the spiders which crawl up the side. His blind, ruthless confidence in his (the Church's) views combined with a disdain for those who fall short of their demands is toxic: 'Love the sinner, hate the sin', as long as the sin is abandoned within his timetable and under his wise counsel. In fact it's more 'Love the sinner if he gives up the sin', love as a reward for good behaviour, by which point the sinner will have become another prig, another prude.

'A spoonful of honey attracts more flies than a barrel full of vinegar,' said St Francis de Sales, but Father Neville adds vinegar to all his jars of honey. Every word he speaks tastes bitter to me. Although I'm sure he means to encourage he ends up bullying, and his rigidity makes it impossible for me to welcome even the inspiring things he might have to say. My spirit plunges down, empty, sucked dry, and from the bottom of the pit I look up in a breathless panic and see only that joyless smile and those clear, grey eyes: 'Just have trust', a last muffled phrase as the lid to the airless chamber snaps shut.

Wristwatch always in view (strapped around a surprisingly fecund fuzz of hair) he leaves after exactly twenty minutes – punctuality is another mortification. Did I notice the slightest limp as he walked towards the door today? Did he want me to know that under the outward cheer he too was suffering a little – for the salvation of souls, for the salvation of my soul?

4 LAZARUS

'How is your prayer life?' Did you like my answer, Father Neville? Ha, I'm no fool. I've read my Tanquerey, my Scaramelli. I know my Purgative Way from my Illuminative Way. I've splashed around in shallower waters too – Merton, Nouwen, Pennington, Keating. I know the lingo. I could write a book on prayer. I've spent years on my knees, eyes closed, heart reaching out for something (trying to pray is praying, they say), but I don't think I've ever really prayed in my life. The practice of my faith has fallen away so easily in these past years, like cheap wrapping paper torn loose on an awkwardly-shaped gift. I convinced you, didn't I, that I was here to intensify a spiritual life which already has prayer at its centre? Did the bishop not fill you in? I've been sent on this retreat because I've been a naughty boy. He is worried about me, my indiscretions, my depression, my addiction, my impending disgrace.

But anyway I'm here, and I'm keeping a journal during these long, silent days. Days of Mass, meditation, examination of conscience . . . 'write it all down as you sit with the Scriptures. Whatever comes to mind. Don't sanitize or edit. Just let the Holy Spirit work with you like clay.' You said this to me yesterday, Father, but do you think it's wise? Do you realize how sticky clay can be? You're an innocent man, I presume, and considerably younger than me. Have you had your 40th birthday yet? I think you're too earnest, too naive to be guiding souls; your hair is too lustrous, your cassock too tell-tale-tidy – the saints have frayed, faded sleeves. And your eyes are too bright, too impatient, too quick to look away, not from me but from yourself.

I doubt you will, but if you ever happen to read these notes in the future I have some advice for you. It will be too late for me, but it may help the next soul who comes to you for direction. Allow time, Father. Time . . . and space. Sometimes (most times) it's better to say nothing. Hear what people are *not* saying. Allow room for their silence when they have more to say than they can bear. And watch that smile. A smile can bring comfort but it can also create a barrier with someone who is in despair. To help a soul like me you have to see yourself as worse than me – and you don't. You think you're holy. Not a saint yet, of course, you are bright enough to know that that would be an instant disqualification for a Christian. Saints think they are sinners, but *real* saints don't think about themselves at all. Aiming for holiness is the surest way to miss it. You think that if you are obedient to your superiors and if you avoid transgression then ... clink: the gate of Heaven will swing open on its golden hinge.

Oh I know I'm being mean and possibly even unfair. I realize that you are a cathedral of holiness next to my pockmarked, concrete tower-block, but your doors are bolted and the bell-tower is silent. I know you're doing what you've been told to do – the will of God, following your vocation, obeying the Church – but you're trapped inside the system as if sealed inside a tomb. And it stinks. 'Lazarus, come forth!' I plan to unwrap some of my own bandages this week. I've got a lot of time on my hands.

5   MEMORARE

Then this morning, another wet, dismal morning, Father Neville brought it up. 'Father, are you having any problems with holy purity?'

'Er ... what do you mean, Father?'

'I mean are you living the virtue of chastity as befits a priest of the Church?' His voice had risen a little. It had taken on a hue of petulance. I really didn't think it was his business to ask me about this, but then I realized it was precisely his business. That's what a director of a retreat is meant to do, to lead the retreatant in self-examination and thus to lead him closer to God. And 'having problems with holy purity' is precisely why I am here.

His voice normalized and he continued, looking at my face but not my eyes.

'A priest who does not live this virtue has fallen at the first post. Nothing he does is of any value if he fails in chastity. God never allows us to be tempted beyond our strength so it should be *impossible to conceive* that a priest would commit a mortal sin in this area.' His hands italicized the words with vehemence. 'He may occasionally give in to the beginnings of lustful thoughts but his habitual state should be to reject them as he would step away from a viper.' He had warmed to the subject and his eyes were shining. 'You must do everything in your power to avoid occasions of sin, any situation where you know you will be tempted. Special care must be taken with the internet and with television... and of course with any unavoidable encounters with women. Be on full alert. The moment you are aware of any giving in to temptation, snuff it out like a candle. Then pray to Our Lady for strength. She is your safest recourse in this area. Do you recite the Memorare?'

'I'm afraid I don't, Father... anymore.' I was simultaneously annoyed and shaken because I had not yet admitted to having problems with sexual matters. Had he guessed? Did every priest have problems in this area so he felt it safe to go on the premeditated attack? And women! The stereotype. The temptress Eve with her golden tresses drawing Adam and the entire human race into sin and condemnation.

Another *memorare* flashed into my mind, my mother in her tight headscarf, fingering her rosary beads, a worried look on her face, saying that very prayer every day. Remember, oh most gracious (*gracious*, the '*a*' rising high in supplication) Virgin Mary . . . never was it known . . . we fly unto thee . . . to thee do we cry . . . sinful and sorrowful . . . despise not our petitions . . . in thy clemency. It was high baroque. High theatre. High camp. Bernini or Caravaggio in words. In fact, seen in this light I began to feel more comfortable with this coloratura prayer's plush, sensual harmonies, its decorative ornamentation tickling the ribs of the tune's skeleton. I no longer saw my mother's anxious Irish face but an Italian stud, tempestuous, incorrigible, wild with passion, mired in sin, capturing then breaking the hearts of every woman and man who crossed his path from puberty to senility, from testicle's descent to prostate's removal.

The Italians make the rules, the Irish keep them . . . as the quip goes. At home and abroad Hibernian spirituality has got it wrong. Catholicism is for the extravagant and for the fallen. It only thrives in the south, under the hot sun, wine and oil spilt on the tablecloth, a slap on the backside of a feisty waitress, wolf-whistles in the town square. Not in the rain and the dripping cold of Craigbourne with Father Neville's pinched lips and ramrod spine and white-chested, flat-nippled prudery. Not Guinness's black and white certainties but the tongue-teasing complexity of a fine Amarone. Thoughts of Bernini and Caravaggio lifted my spirits.

He was still talking. 'Pay particular attention to this area, Father Joseph. Not only your own soul but the souls of those under your care rely on your efforts here. Mortification. Crucify the flesh. And Our Lady. As I've mentioned, she will be your ally in the battle for purity.' Well, I love the gentle Jewish girl from Nazareth, and I love the strong Jewish woman at Calvary, but heaven preserve me from the worried headscarves and furrowed brows of the Irish women of my youth.

Shifting a little on his hard chair Father Neville asked, 'Are there any women in your life, your housekeeper, a parishioner perhaps, who could be an occasion of sin for you?'

'No, Father Neville.' I paused and looked him straight in the eye. 'I'm gay.' He winced, whether at the very idea of homo-sexuality ('He who lived with the vice of sodomy suffers more in Hell than others for this is the greatest sin' – thank you, St Bernadine of Siena!) or at my easy use of the playful, modern, accepting three-letter word. The awkward moment passed and he smiled again.

'God bless you, Father Joseph.' He stood up. 'We'll meet again tomorrow morning.'

'When did you first realize that you had same-sex attraction?' asked Father Neville today. Where do I start? Out of the mists of infancy, as each year passed, my preference for boys gradually became clearer and stronger. Classmates at primary school, the teenager who delivered the newspapers, my swimming instructor, television personalities, film stars, the young gardener at the large house on the main road, summer sweat, shirt peeled off, wheelbarrow biceps . . . shall I go on? It's simple: with self-consciousness came the consciousness of same-sex attraction.

Patrick, my fellow altar boy, was my first serious crush. I was nine and he was ten when we began to serve Saturday morning Mass together. He was tall for his age, strong, sporty, confident, clever. I used to stand behind him in the sacristy after Mass, close so I could smell his body and look up at the nape of his neck. I wanted to take care of him, to protect him. Couldn't we make a home somewhere, a place where we would always be together? At church it was our job to put away all the utensils from the service, linens, books, candles, cruets, paten, chalice. It was cool inside the sacristy and I loved the mingle of his smell with the smell of the polish and the incense. I could have stayed there for hours. No lingering after Mass for him though. He couldn't wait to get out of there, tearing off his surplice and flinging open the back door, out into the hot morning, flies buzzing in the sun, grass long and shining, day's youth sprung underfoot. 'Let's go and play football, Joe,' he'd say, racing ahead with one shoelace undone, his hair like tumbled hay. I would chase after him and admire his grace as he loped along, the rudder of his shirt flapping loose.

I loved him, even if I didn't understand the word, even if I couldn't name it. I wrote his name over and over again in my exercise book and always with a blush of pleasure. I would then scratch it out in case anyone saw, or rip out the page and tear it into a hundred pieces, but a day or so later I'd write it all over again. We were inseparable and when his family moved away I felt devastated, with an emptiness inside but also something sickly, like an open wound.

A couple of weeks before they left he was over at my house and we were playing at being priests. We got some old curtain material from the bottom of my mother's wardrobe and rigged it up to look like two chasubles. Then we set up an altar in my bedroom with a missal, two candles and a crucifix. After processing into the room in solemn silence we began our fake liturgy. Then it happened. At one point he moved next to me, very close. I could feel his breath against my face. Then he kissed my cheek. It was as if a bolt of electricity had struck me, my childish fingers pushed into a live socket. The whole religious world we had created in my bedroom melted away like wax. It seemed like a silly, childish game, a mirage replaced in a flash by the reality of flesh. I turned to him and our lips met, two boys in taffeta drapery fumblingly experiencing the dawn of physical intimacy. And then, just seconds later, that new world itself melted away as we both woke up to the discomfort of the situation. We had glimpsed adulthood and we were not ready for it, slamming the door closed as if to contain a raging furnace. We were kids again. We blushed, now out of embarrassment rather than desire.

'I've got to go,' Patrick said, hurriedly removing the fake vestments and flinging them on to the bed. 'I'll see you around, Joe...'

He ran down the stairs and out the front door, his footsteps clattering down the path. I heard the gate open and then heard it bang shut. I stood for a moment in silence in my bedroom, still draped in the curtain material, feeling desperately lonely. Then I blew out the candles and slowly started to put away the liturgical decorations. His guilty, dirty departure was devastating for me. He was my best friend and I feared I'd lost him for ever. We'd promised to write after he moved away but he never replied to my long, slightly feverish letters. In fact, I never saw or heard from him again after that fumbled kiss in front of the makeshift altar.

7   MASTURBATION

Patrick was the overture but then I discovered masturbation, that solo aria with, for a Catholic boy, its inexorable crescendo of guilt. My youthful conscience was me, and it condemned me. An ingrowing toenail of moral failure. It started one bath time – it was winter. The air in the freezing room was a thick mist. The too-hot water was scalding my body. My hands, their fingers mottled into Braille-like lumps, were swishing underneath. I stretched out, full-length, hair wet with suds, neck red, chin flushed. Then hands smoothed across chest, under arms, down legs, brushed against…away. Then again. A dusting past. Away (briefer this time) then a firm swish, left knee raised, water splashing up the side of the tub, shoulders shrugged back into the bubbles, then another brush. But stopping now. And holding. A swollen pink buoy on the surface of the water. Then quickly away. A stretch. Then slowly back. Knee down. Then hand across the foam then touching then holding. Then holding tighter. And now rubbing a few times, then away, into the soapy froth, a foot raised to the cold tap's still-cold metal, its big toe inserted into the limescale hole.

The ceiling, looking up at the ceiling. Where was I? A stranger in my house; everything familiar but changed (down and up, down). What the hell was I feeling? (Held.) A glow like nothing I'd ever felt (and up), a motion as natural as the heart beating. I was sweating even though by now the water was lukewarm and the bubbles almost gone. (Down.) The condensation on the ceramic wall-tiles was trickling down. (Up.) Yellow streetlights outside shining through the frosted window. Inside (down-up-down-up) the towel hanging unevenly from the radiator (down) and then…then…then the towel falling then the condensation a river then the light outside exploding then some strange liquid gushing heart pounding throbbing head flushed flustered guilt gusting. My head was out of the shell. I had come of age. I had burst into adulthood. But then a strange lurch backwards: I was an infant again. Abandoned on a doorstep one minute then in the next breath as if suffocated with cloying motherly protection. A re-attached umbilical cord. The disturbing contradictions of puberty's wrestle, both clinging and repelling in the same placenta-licking embrace. I was a chicken wriggling out of an egg, a wallaby leaving the pouch; my foreskin covering then exposing an unbearably sensitive, ecstatic penis.

It was a one-off. 'I'll never do that again.' Its power terrified me. I'd opened a box and I quickly closed it. But I knew where the box lay. I could go to look at it without danger, couldn't I? I could touch the surface, confident that the key was in the lock, turned firmly to the right. I could even touch the key, turn it further to the right, play with the tassel hanging from the keyring. But in my bed, in my dreams, the box began to open up in front of me of its own accord. It spilled its contents on to my sheets. And eventually I began to open the box myself, to leave it unlocked, to carry it with me, to keep it always by my side.

8 JASON

Into my early teens masturbation fed then sated my sexual desires; its repetitive constancy became a muffled mantra in the Confessional. Often I thought I would choke when I spluttered out yet again the M word to the shadow of a priest hidden behind the curtain. I was on a constant knife-edge of guilt, but sex was something experienced alone, always alone – the solitary sin, the secret midnight raid of the fridge. Others did not enter my erogenous zone. There were crushes along the way but these were simply crushed. If you think you're going to Hell if you fool around sexually with another person . . . well, that's a bucket of iced water carried on your shoulders into every situation. It became a reflex: I'd see an attractive man, I'd instantly recall that this was a temptation from the Devil, I'd mumble a quick prayer, I'd finger my rosary beads, then . . . whoosh! A dousing. The powers of Hell thwarted. The Devil defeated. But it slowly turned sick, turned for me into the only thing I thought about: sex was sin was sex was hell was sex. The constant possibility of falling into such an abyss is to be constantly walking on the crumbling edge of a cliff. Such continence requires a forceful diversion of a natural human pipeline and can result in geysers gushing out of sight, out of control. There are some men who seem to manage it but I don't know if such self-control is physiological or supernatural. So clear seems their vision and so all-encompassing their dedication and so strong their will that . . . and yet. Perhaps their geysers are simply further away. In my mid-teens things began to change. I started to think more seriously about the priesthood and I stopped jerking off. I reached 17, pimples not too bad after a year or two of gangle and gauche, then off to the seminary – or rather the novitiate.

The Oblates of Christ is a small religious order founded in Naples in the early 19th century. It was languishing when Father Mario Tetrazzini, one of their few remaining priests and a friend of the then Archbishop of Illinois, went to Chicago in Lent 1978 to preach a Mission in a poor, inner-city parish. Certain healings took place during his eight-day stay, most remarkably a woman in a wheelchair who at the moment of Holy Communion on the first morning simply stood up and haltingly, but without help, walked up to the altar rail to receive the Host from Father Mario. There was understandably a tremendous buzz amongst those in the congregation. As the week progressed other miracles were reported and the queue outside his Confessional grew to hundreds of people. By the end of the week an intense fervour had taken root. The church was filled from morning to night, the Blessed Sacrament exposed, candles burning, tears flowing, vocations forming.

In addition to working miracles Father Mario preached a strong, conservative message in his strong, Italian accent. He fulminated against abortion, homosexuality, contraception, secularism, lukewarmness, liturgical abuse, neglect of the Blessed Virgin, disobedience to the Pope, Modernism – bullet points in his fiery sermons going straight to the heart and ricocheting back to Rome where the recently-installed John Paul II was about to begin a spring-cleaning, sweeping away the mess left by his predecessor, the indecisive, melancholy Paul VI. John Paul was not a conventional conservative but he was happy to endorse whoever was loyal and obedient. Over the next years Father Mario became a cult-like figure, with hundreds of fervent young men joining the Order of which he was now Superior General. He came to Manchester to preach in 1981 and I went to hear him with my mother. She adored him; he was absolutely her sort of priest. He heard my Confession and I couldn't deny the magnetism of his charisma. He was exhilarating, tough, uncompromising. Later that evening my mother came out with it: 'I see that Father Mario has opened an English-speaking novitiate in Chicago.' She didn't need to say any more, and that summer I flew to the United States and joined the Oblates of Christ as a 19-year-old novice.

But within a few months of being there I felt hopelessly out of place. My fellow novices (all nine of them) were narrow-minded and prudish. There was a hothouse atmosphere, a competitive spirituality as to who could spend longest in the chapel, who could be up earliest, who could be most abstemious at the dinner table, who could stay longest praying after Communion. The talk during recreation times was narrow and bigoted. It was the start of the AIDS epidemic and cruel, ignorant remarks were commonplace. One of the nine was a little more sympathetic and we became friends – Jason from the Philippines. A stocky, short guy with dark skin and a big smile who tried to appear macho-tough but was actually quite sensitive. He was musically inclined and his tuneful, powerful singing voice always rose above the others in the chapel services.

One spring day the two of us were assigned to paint the recreation room whilst the other novices were outside doing work in the grounds. Devoid of charm and with insufficient furniture to fill its cavernous space (a man in a suit too big for him), this room was where we had our community get-togethers and where we occasionally watched movies – Bing Crosby's *Bells of St Mary's*, Hitchcock's *I Confess*, Mickey Rooney's *Boystown*, but also videos of Father Mario preaching (*sempre con fuoco*) with subtitles. There was an upright piano in the corner which I had played a few times but which was now covered with dust sheets. Jason was sanding the wall near it when he came across some music scores on a shelf – mainly songs from the shows *Carousel*, *My Fair Lady*, *South Pacific*.

'Hey Joe, I used to sing these back in the Philippines. Shall we try one? What about this?' I put down my paintbrush and walked over to the piano as he opened the book at 'I've Grown Accustomed to Her Face' – Lerner and Lowe, that alliterative dream-team of melody and romance. I uncovered the piano, balanced the score on its rickety desk, and sat down to vamp the introduction, my eyes darting up and down awkwardly from music to keyboard. Then he began to sing, standing behind me quite closely, bending over a little, obviously needing to read the words from the page. He sang pretty well, although I got the feeling that he was more interested in projecting the vibration of his vocal chords than the emotions of the song. Indeed the volume increased as he got carried away and I was scared that

Brother Dominic would return and hear us – but I didn't like to discourage him.

He turned the page and I could smell his breath and his clean, black hair as he leant over me. 'Ac-cust-omed to her . . . ' – four B flats, each with a slightly different tuning from his untrained, youthful voice. This vocal blip alongside his cockiness made him seem vulnerable and strangely irresistible. My heart began to beat faster.

'That sounds great, Jason,' I said as he finished. 'Let's try another. What about "You'll Never Walk Alone"?' I felt safer in C major and this time the melody's arch was higher and more passionate. He put his hand on my shoulder as he began and I started to tremble, my fingers suddenly cold and moist. He really got into it and it was pretty loud in my ear. Then his hand on my shoulder became his leg against my back as he began the second verse. His vanity, his fondness for his own voice, was the guard he had let down, and I found myself carried along the river in a swift and dangerous current. I was on the point of stopping, of saying that we should get back to work, of dousing myself with that bucket of iced water which was ready on my shoulder (there was enough for both of us), but I delayed. I allowed the romantic moment to unfold. I kept playing, he kept singing, his arm now around my shoulder as if we were two leads on Broadway. That's it! We're actors! It's theatre! We're on stage! This isn't reality! This can't be sin!

We finished the song and there was a strange pause. It seemed to last a minute but was probably only a few seconds.

We looked at each other, inside each other. The music had ended in silence and only a bird now sang outside the window. I was on fire. He was flushed too and was smiling his big, white grin. I'd not been aware of any special sexual attraction to Jason before, but now with the music and the hand and the leg and the gaze of our eyes I was overcome with tenderness and desire. He quickly leant towards me and kissed my lips, but in a stagey, jokey kind of way, as if to break a spell rather than to cast one.

'Thanks Joe,' he said breezily. 'You play really well. Hey, we should get on with the decorating if we're going to finish before Benediction.' He moved away and started vigorously rubbing the sander against the wall, his back to me. I was speechless, my throat tight, my feelings confused. I had a full erection and my whole body was hot. 'Thanks Joe' were sweet words from a mouth I wanted to kiss again, but also words of cancellation, of erasure, of a return to normality. And words of a certain hauteur, as if I'd done him a favour, a rental pianist for his audition, a jobbing accompanist sitting out of view whilst he flaunted himself before the producer and director, hungry for the role, desperate for fame. I was both attracted by and resentful of his ego. Irrationally, I felt used by him, sexually and musically, but I longed for it to happen again. I wanted him to kiss me deep and long and hard . . . and I needed to go to Confession.

No one to confess to except Father Pietro, our spiritual director, the resident priest. Would Jason also go to Confession? Would he think he'd sinned? Maybe such a gesture of affection, such fooling-around, was customary for Filipinos back home, much like Italian men who throw their arms around each other whilst wolf-whistling at passing pretty girls. I didn't know what Jason would do and there was no way on earth I could talk to him about it, but I knew I had sinned. I'd felt the passion. I could have stopped the intimate moment but I didn't. It had given me intense physical pleasure. I knew it at the time but I continued, and I would do it all over again. Then the waves of panic began. If I would do it again then I was not repentant. Yes, if Jason had put down the sander and walked over to me and taken me in his arms and thrust his tongue to the back of my teeth I would have offered no resistance.

I was shaking and my mind was spinning. Contrition was out of the question, but maybe attrition was possible, repentance through fear of Hell rather than love of God? My heart was beating quickly again, but now not from desire. I had to go to Confession as soon as possible. I was in a state of mortal sin. If the room we were in were suddenly to catch fire and the blaze to spread wildly and consume the sofas and the books and the piano then roar ferociously towards me engulfing me in seconds in a screaming heap of flames... then I would go to the flames of Hell for all eternity. Hell for all eternity. If you travelled to the Sahara and began to count every grain of sand in that desert, taking one minute for each grain, when you finished it would be as if only day one in that place of torment where you were destined to spend so many days that the number of zeros would themselves be like the grains of sand under your burning feet. That is the teaching of the Church, unadulterated by flabby liberalism or equivocating modernism. One kiss between two men in which the pleasure found was not repudiated and resisted was enough to land you in the Sahara desert on a one-way ticket. And me? I was sitting on the piano bench wanting to feel those Filipino lips press against my mouth again.

We were silent for the next half-hour as we continued our decorating. Benediction was at 5:00 and at 4:30 Brother Dominic popped his head in the door.

'OK guys, you should get yourselves cleaned up now. You've done a good job here. Looking nice.' Jason put down his sander and walked out jauntily whilst I held back a little. 'Brother Dominic?' I said, as Jason disappeared around the corner. 'I need to see Father Pietro. Is . . . is he around?'

'Yeah, I saw him go up to his room, Joe. But there's not enough time to see him before Benediction. Go and have a shower now and you can talk to him after dinner.'

I hurried out of the room, still hoping that I could manage to see the priest before the service began, but I couldn't do so as I was, covered with paint and dust and dirt. I raced up the stairs to my room, grabbed a towel, and went to the bathroom to take a quick shower before getting into my cassock. It was now 4:50. I still had 10 minutes. I walked over to Father Pietro's room and knocked on his door. There was no answer. I knocked again. Again, no answer. I was still in a state of panic and so I ran back down the stairs to the chapel and saw him talking to one of the Brothers outside the sacristy. I walked up slowly, looking down at my feet, hoping he would see me and finish his conversation but staying far enough away so that it didn't look like I was eavesdropping. Eventually the Brother turned and walked away and the priest went directly into the room where he would vest for the liturgy, seeming not to have noticed me. I followed him into the darkened space. 'Father,' I called out. He stopped and turned around. It was now just a couple of minutes before five o'clock. 'Can I have a word?' Then I added in a quieter voice, 'I need to go to Confession.'

'Well, there's no time now, Joe. Benediction starts in a couple of minutes.' I felt sick, guilty, filthy. 'Come and see me in the sacristy after the service.'

I went into the chapel and knelt down. There was Jason on the other side, head bowed, seemingly at peace. I suddenly felt like an outsider. I felt as if I had crashed not a party but an intimate family gathering. I had opened the door and entered inside and taken a seat where the children should be sitting. The parents themselves were kind and gracious but I knew I had sat down where I did not belong. A bell rang and Father Pietro, covered in a gorgeous bejewelled cope, entered the sanctuary from the right side, genuflected slowly and reverently, then removed the Host from the tabernacle and placed it in the bright gold monstrance. He positioned it carefully on the altar, perfectly centred, and genuflected again, with a sigh of devotion and with eyes fixed on the white wafer inside the glass case. No, this was not like crashing another family's gathering but instead as if an invisible wall had arisen between me and my own family, cast out, disgraced, stripped of my place at the table. During the hymns and chants of the service I could hear Jason's voice riding over the rest of us and it made me feel a searing melancholy which came directly from my churning stomach.

After Benediction I went again to the sacristy where Father Pietro was disrobing.

'Father...'

'Yes, I know, Joe. You want to go to Confession. Just wait a minute.' His brusqueness surprised me. He seemed impatient and annoyed. Wasn't he meant to welcome the return of a sinner? My courage was already faltering. Had Jason already been to see him whilst I was taking my shower? What had he said, if so? No, there wouldn't have been time. Was I putting Jason in an awkward position by mentioning him in this context? Well, I didn't need to name him. I could just say that I'd had a sexual encounter with another man. But who else could it have been, seeing as I hadn't left the premises? But saying I'd had a sexual encounter was stupid. It sounded much worse than it was, like we'd actually had sex. Yet why should it bother me if the priest thought worse of me? My sin was as bad as if we'd fucked for an hour on top of the altar. A mortal sin is a mortal sin. The Sahara. And being ashamed of telling Father Pietro was pride, another sin. It didn't matter what the priest thought of me, whether he was impressed or not. Or did it? Could this stop my being ordained? Would he remember this for ever, even feel compelled to mention it to Father Tetrazzini himself? No, he couldn't do that because all that is mentioned in Confession is kept secret. But he could voice concerns about my vocation, about my suitability, without naming them. And what would my mother say if I were to be rejected from the Oblates of Christ? My heart froze as Father Pietro continued to disrobe, these thoughts tumbling around in my head in a frenzied cacophony.

And then I had a brainwave. I would simply say to him that I had entertained sexual thoughts and taken pleasure in them. That *was* the sin after all. Two human beings placing their lips together for one second was not the sin. The sin was in the mind – not as in imaginary but as in internal consent. 'You have heard that it was said to them of old: Thou shalt not commit adultery. But I say to you, that whosoever shall look on a woman to lust after her, hath already committed adultery with her in his heart.' That's it! I can spare Jason, I can avoid misunderstanding, I can be truthful (in a real, spiritual sense), and I can get absolved. I felt an instant, tremendous relief, and it became a technique I used frequently over the years. 'Entertained sexual thoughts' – a hostess throwing supper parties, no shortage of guests.

'Do you have any recurring temptations of an impure nature?' asked Father Pietro when I first applied to join the Oblates of Christ.

'No, Father,' I replied. It was an honest answer in that I was convinced such temptations were firmly under my control. Before deciding to enter the novitiate my reflex of avoiding occasions of sin with others had become honed and habitual and I had even stopped masturbating. At night inside the bedclothes if I felt an erection developing I would reach for my rosary and start to meditate on the Sorrowful Mysteries. Almost immediately the excitement would dissipate and I would imagine myself under the loving gaze of my Guardian Angel. I didn't have to deal with the jaws of sin because my temptations had baby teeth. There are other sins of course, not just those of the flesh, but these didn't figure in my thoughts. They seemed even easier dragons to slay – toothless wonders in thrall to the One True Church.

But I probably should have told him about my steady stream of wet dreams. Sometimes my sheets were barely dry from last night's emission when I found myself soaked again, trembling with guilt in the aftermath of my body's exploding pressure cooker. Great wet patches through pyjamas to the mattress were seedbeds sufficient for nations, their stains like continents mapped out on the linens of my bed. Sometimes I woke up on the very edge of an orgasm and thrust my engines into reverse with fervent prayer. My heart was racing and my loins were aching and I felt a frightening surge of panic: had I sinned? Could I receive Communion before going to Confession? If I didn't receive Communion what would people think? No one denies themselves the Sacrament because of an angry word or a jealous thought. No, when you see that young man staying back in the pew when others are going forward and everyone is singing 'Sweet Sacrament Divine', it's sex sex sex.

No one had ever really talked to me about sex. I'd discovered my own source of secret pleasure with masturbation, mined it frequently for a few years, then blocked it, gas safely turned off at the mains . . . until the later explosion. At least girls have to have explained to them what is happening as they begin their monthly periods, but with boys it can all go unspoken, information gleaned from behind a shed, in a bubble-gum whisper, in a mutual fumble when peeing in the toilets, a knowing smirk from a pubescent fuzz-face, cunts and slits and dicks and cum and balls. Sex was something from which I shut my ears. The rubbish dump of fucking and a contented, rosy-cheeked family gathered around the hearth . . . there could be no possible connection between these two images in my youthful mind.

10   GOLD CUFFLINKS

Sitting here at my desk my mind keeps going back to that year at Immaculate Heart in Chicago, a quarter of a century ago. That year of exploring then rejecting a vocation with the Oblates of

Christ. What a contrast to Craigbourne! Immaculate Heart was clean and bright – and the water pressure! I'd never stood under an American shower before then and I couldn't believe the torrent of hot water that covered my body on that first morning. I felt guilty enjoying such a sensual moment but that was short-lived because Father Pietro recommended that we take cold showers for mortification. Then the gushing was less welcome, although still better than the piddling, hand-held shower we'd had at home, its tubes a toothless blow-job around the taps. Edging our stained bath tub was a floppy, mildewed curtain which would slap against me in a flap of annoyance, as disgusting as an elderly aunt's wet kiss. After my drafty childhood bathroom Chicago was paradise.

We didn't get to see much of the city as we were stuck out in Joliet, but on two occasions we were driven to magnificent St Peter's Cathedral for Mass with the Archbishop of Illinois. Cardinal O'Reilly was an impressive man on many levels. Tall with a large frame and an athletic build, he was jovial in a way that seemed to facilitate his keeping a distance from you rather than drawing you closer to him. His friendly pat on the back and chortling laugh was a practised way to leave a situation behind, not to invite a confidence. I know that busy men like him need these techniques for quick exits along fast-track lanes, but once you've noticed that it's a technique the smiles and the bonhomie seem hollow and they fail to cheer. Not like Bishop Bernard whose shyness calms and consoles; he wouldn't have lasted the length of a Novena in the bustle of the dioceses of Chicago or

New York or Los Angeles. The Cardinal's polished Cadillac, his chunky gold cufflinks, his crisp white shirts, his crisp white hair – a Prince of the Church on his throne in the mission fields of North America. He ran a tight ship, all polished brass and rich-hued oak, it's just that I could never imagine Christ walking up its gangplank to preach. No, the Nazarene was to be seen standing with sandalled feet in a fishing boat, floor dank with stale brine and fish bones: 'But what went ye out for to see? A man clothed in soft raiment? Behold, they that wear soft clothing are in kings' houses.' The Cardinal's residence was the only king's house I've ever visited.

Because he venerated our own Father Tetrazzini we were treated very well. After Mass there was a brunch at the splendid Palmer House hotel, built in the days when Wall Street seemed indestructible. Its lobby was dazzling, an opulent secular cathedral where the Sunday sacrament was smoked salmon and champagne rather than bread and wine, accompanied by the groove of grainy live jazz in place of choir boys and organ. It was my first Sunday in America, barely over the jet lag, eating French toast (French?) with maple syrup and blueberries (what was maple syrup? What were blueberries?), eggs over-easy (so easy) and bacon crisped in snap-crackle slabs. Air-conditioned, airbrushed, air-headed – thrilling and totally overwhelming after Timperley and Tescos. And yet that kind of confident, glossy American Catholicism made my experience with the Oblates worse in the long run. It was all so fake. To mortify myself on a deep-pile blue carpet, to reach around to whip my back whilst vents blew temperature-controlled air into the welts, to reduce my intake of food when there was a choice of half-and-half, full fat, or semi-skimmed milk... it all seemed like amateur theatre, complete with bad make-up, ill-fitting costumes and overacting. I just couldn't take it seriously. Serious though was the smug self-satisfaction which such self-denial bred in some of us. Soon we were to learn that the costume of our black habits was a sign that we had been set apart, that we were experts-in-training for higher things. Callow youths as vessels of grace with easy answers for every difficult question.

11   ALTRINCHAM AGAIN

After about six months with the Oblates I knew I had to leave. It was not just the episode with Jason, although that unsettled me; in such a small community it was intolerable to have something like that unacknowledged yet present in every unavoidable encounter. After our Broadway moment our friendship cooled. He would always sit apart from me at meals or recreation and he would make sure we were never on the same roster to serve Mass. When I passed him in the corridors he would look away with a tight smile, quickening his step. Actually I don't think he was gay – he ended up getting married and moving back to the Philippines. No, it wasn't to avoid the 'occasions of sin' that led him to avoid me but rather his wounded sense of pride and shame. The macho image he had formed of himself had been shattered in the soar of a show tune. Like many men from cultures where a man's manliness is central to his identity, the perceived effeminacy of same-sex intimacy was repellent to him. Our kiss had taken the wind out of the sails of his self-esteem in one fabulous puff. An anonymous one-night stand was one thing, a condom flushed down the toilet, forgotten or denied in the haze of too many beers, but a sober daylight kiss with someone whom you then saw constantly in a setting of avowed celibacy was a perpetual humiliation.

But aside from the episode with Jason I began to hate the small, stuffy world of Immaculate Heart, the rigidity of everything, the military organization, the unwavering belief that everything was exactly as God wanted: 'The rule of the Oblates of Christ is not to be changed. It represents the perfect will of God for those called into its community.' And then the idolization of Father Mario sickened me. Once a week in the recreation room we would have to watch a video of his sermon from the previous Sunday. We were encouraged to take notes, to select one point he made and use it for our daily meditation the following week. Our own living Saint from Naples, his photo in every room, his name on everyone's lips, even his mother's photo in the dining room, always with a freshly-cut rose (her favourite flower) in a vase under the image. Humans love leaders, strong leaders, and soon we make them into kings, and then the kings start believing in their divine right to be kings. 'The Father', we were meant to call him. 'Call no one on earth your father. You have one Father in Heaven.' Wise words from a wise Man.

I dragged my heels for a few more months but at the end of my first year in Chicago I returned to England, to train as a secular priest for the diocese of Altrincham.

12   BUBBLE BURST

I was destined to be a priest from the moment the doctor cut my umbilical cord and exclaimed to my mother, 'It's a beautiful baby boy.' Seeing a pink penis halfway down the slimy torso meant that, for her, I was already consecrated to the Lord. She would do everything in her power from that moment on to make my path to priesthood smooth, and inevitable. In front of the statue of St Joseph, paint peeling off the yellowing lily he held in his right hand, a candle was lit each early morning before the 7:30 Mass. 'Make my son a priest; give him a vocation to the holy priesthood,' my mother would plead, as the match scratched a bright flame from the blackened sandpaper and set alight the waxy wick.

I was born into a bubble of religion. Life's instruction manual was a battered prayerbook. Days were punctuated with signs of the cross, splashes of holy water, kissing of Miraculous Medals, the rattle of rosaries and the noontime recitation of the Angelus as the clock-hands met at the top of the dial. I learned early on that if I behaved well I would be rewarded with a caress, a smile; if not, there would be a palpable withholding of affection and occasionally a sharp slap. When I grew older every aspect of my behaviour was scrutinized, then praised or punished by the standard of the saints. A careless genuflection would receive a cold, disappointed look; a head bowed low in prayer after Holy Communion a satisfied smile. I knew I could make my mother happy with certain words and certain actions, and that made *me* happy, an habitual if neurotic chain of cause and effect.

By the time I was a teenager the hints were heavy: 'Why don't you go on this retreat? We could catch the evening Mass in town. So many souls remain in Purgatory because there is no one to pray for them. Did you read that biography of Maximilian Kolbe I gave you? What are you giving up for Lent? Have you been to Confession this month? Do you want to talk to Fr Murphy? The visiting priest at St Monica's is a Benedictine; they know how to pray, the Benedictines.' How could I not become a priest? Everything in our house was related to the Church, from the holy water stoop by the front door ('Bless This House') to Our Lady in a huge frame in our living room, her foot pushed against the head of a writhing serpent as she watched television with us.

My ordination was the happiest day of my life because it was the happiest day of my mother's life, her ultimate approval. I had passed the final test. A man wearing a freshly-pressed black cassock with a brilliant-white starched slit at his throat stood before her as she knelt for a blessing. It was a momentous moment for me too – the look of reverential awe on her face, the instant authority I had in the community despite being a young man whose only experience of the wider world was a trip to Lourdes in his teens and a year in the novitiate in Illinois.

So how did I get from that first Mass – newly-ordained hands wet with oil, mother's cheeks wet with tears – to my first prostitute? I don't want to write about it. I don't want to map that journey in my memory. Before and after is easier: that was me, this is me; but the transition is a blurred dream I don't wish to recall or interpret. Those years of outward observance, faith seemingly unfluttered, doctrines confidently preached – was it all a fake, a shell? After my mother's death the shell finally fell away, but how could it have happened so quickly?

When I first left the Oblates of Christ and began training for the diocesan priesthood I certainly let things become laxer. I still prayed but in a loose, carefree kind of way. Nevertheless I was happy and content as a seminarian and then as a priest. But the years passed and my lukewarm life began to feel dreary and tasteless. The outer novelty of it wore off and it felt as if I were perpetually stuck at a dinner party with people who bored me. No escape, conversation dry and pointless to left and right.

Then, during the three years of my mother's dementia, I began experimenting. The occasional half-glances at soft porn websites became a daily habit, and then the porn got harder and the glances got longer. A good twenty bookmarks were saved on my browser and I could spend hours clicking from one orgasm to another. When I first began to open my eyes and my heart to sex it was as if a light had flooded a dark room, as if a shot of brandy had been added to a flavourless cup of coffee. And now, five years after my mother's death, I find myself living inside a womb of perpetual desire. I am fuelled by sexual stimulation, utterly consumed by lust, devoured, ravished by it. Any second of the day or night I'm ready.

How does a building with fine, healthy beams allow its first worm to make a home there, one hole burrowing deep to decay? Was Jason in Illinois my first worm? Or was the gradual easing of observance the warp which led to the complete collapse of the structure of my spiritual life? Was my eventual immersion in sex a way to hide from my faltering faith (swimming underwater to avoid facing the doubts, muting them, choking them), or have my sexual excesses themselves destroyed my faith, eroding its foundations as a coastline recedes with the surge of the tide and the swimmer fails to return to shore?

But now, jaded and tired, sex is more like an injection of heroin into a collapsed vein. I know that the constant plunge from the heights of pleasure to the barren path below is false and ephemeral, but I've become addicted to my stimulated life. It's occasionally ecstatic and occasionally despairing but mostly it's just quietly disappointing, quietly lonely, quietly weary. I have no regrets. I even have a touch of whimsy. But I know that I'm moving in a slow trickle toward oblivion . . . or worse.

The monastic rule, even in an adapted, secular form, is a brace over weakened joints, or perhaps more like a metal rod inside a wounded leg. If I'd been able to walk that demanding path, asking no questions, observant, obedient, my destination (Heaven) would be assured – or so the spiritual directors assure us. The traditional Catholic devotional method in its simple rigidity has been honed over centuries of saints. It sidesteps human nature by imposing a framework that is beyond it. It seeks to replace it with an unmoving, unyielding, indestructible titanium plate hidden under the flesh. But in too many cases the frame supports a decomposing limb, all gore and gangrene. We must fall down to be fully human . . . and then get up again. Too often the canonized saints appear to have walked on stilts.

13   FATHER'S DEATH

My father died on his honeymoon. My mother never spoke to me about it except in the vaguest terms, but when she died I came across some letters and newspaper clippings which she had kept, hidden at the back of a drawer. I discovered that I owed my existence to a 12-hour window. On the second day of their intended week-long stay in Rome my father stepped out in front of a bus, in front of her eyes. The tragedy was reported in the local Italian newspapers and also in the UK press. There was an official letter from the Roman police, another letter of condolence from the traumatized driver, another from the bus company, and then a long, rather enigmatic letter from a priest whom they had known in Manchester and who was in Rome at the time, teaching at the Venerable English College.

Monsignor Thomas Crabbe was an old man when I tracked him down after my mother died. He was living in a nursing home in Prestatyn and was confused about everything, but as I talked to him about this terrible event my intuition that my father's death might have been suicide was strengthened. One night of lovemaking, an abortive breakfast stroll, and then my mother's lifetime of mental distress. I had always imagined that for her the idea of sex had been a necessary evil, that physical intimacy was a distasteful distraction from things of the spirit, that she really belonged in a convent, but as Msgr Crabbe talked about her he became animated:

'Your mother ... lively, pretty. Yes, she ... laughing always laughing. Very happy woman.' He was laughing himself at the memory. 'And with your father. Lovebirds ... so romantic. They were always ... holding, always holding hands. At Communion too.'

This portrait of my mother was as much of a shock to me as the possibility of my father's suicide had been. Occasionally at Christmas after one sherry too many she could get giggly and silly, but that she was a pretty woman with strong romantic impulses who was remembered for her laughter and easy physical intimacy by a priest half a century later – it didn't seem plausible. My recall is of someone pale and serious, making the sign of the cross, gazing towards the picture of the Virgin with a pained expression on her face as if weighed down by the sins of the world. She was always so sober, so fragile, so frightened, so quick to quench my high spirits, to tamp down my immature enthusiasms, to bring down to earth the crazy kites of my childish fantasies. Everything with her was diluted, as if merriment and joy would be used up if we indulged in them too often. She lived on the penultimate page of life's ration book.

I couldn't get a direct answer from confused Msgr Crabbe about my father except general comments about him being a 'quiet, thoughtful man', so I tried to trick the truth out of him: 'How soon did my mother recover after the suicide? Was there a problem with the funeral because my father took his own life?' Eventually (it took an hour of gentle pestering) he told me what he knew. Of course there could be no proof, but my mother had described to him how, as she stood smiling at her husband that morning on the curb waiting to cross the road, she saw something in his eyes as he looked back at her – blind panic, horror, fear, infinite sadness. He looked away then looked back, parted his lips, trembling, as if to say something or to cry out but then, with perfect timing, ran out into the path of an oncoming bus. Death was instantaneous but messy, blood splattered everywhere, an arm partly separated from his torso. She saw it happen, the bang and squelch, the chaos of the traffic, the screams of the passengers, the driver's agonized stare, the surface of the road like a butcher's block.

She never recovered. She lived her whole life as if a virtual vehicle were coming at her from the side, about to crash and pulp her to brains and liver and onions. She never went abroad again. She hid behind a headscarf, her resentment towards

God suppressed into religious practice, a reflex of love/hate/ fear propelling a life stuffed with Masses and rosary beads. She found consolation not in Catholicism but in its caricature – a joyless, pathological religious observance. Then nine months after my father was smeared on the streets of Rome I was smeared across the sheets of an Altrincham hospital – my arrival a bloody reminder of his bloody departure. I was the flesh of my father salvaged from the accident. His ejaculation, all that was still alive of him, had been sleeplessly at work inside her, creating a new life.

14 MORNINGS

A plastic alarm clock. By the bedside. Battery-operated. Yellowing case. Ticking. Not the plum-rounded sound of a wind-up clock but the relentless step of the second hand's shuffling, synthetic circle. This leads me either to a troubling meditation on 'every tick a second closer to death' or it facilitates a comforting, New Age rumination on life's universal pulse. Some mornings at Craigbourne I am able to relax into a holding pattern as the birdsong outside my window weaves an intricate cadenza over the rhythm of the ticking. But more often the two seem separate: I am inside, a prisoner counting the seconds of a life sentence; the birds are outside, flying free, singing, rejoicing. There have been many mystical references made to birdsong as a form of praising God – St Francis of Assisi and the composer Olivier Messiaen come to mind. But on the good mornings birds are my atheist buddies. Their repetitive cries speak of nothing but the air we breathe, and the dew shaken off their wings suggests a world beyond Baptism – ignorant of guilt, soaring above the breeze.

The snooze button gets much use, left palm pulled out of my musky pyjamas to slap to silence the strident alarm. I am usually awake already, snuggled down between the thin sheets, hands drawing warmth (both in body and libido) from around my groin. Early Mass. Out of bed. Bare feet on the grit of the wooden floor. Padding over to the corner: yes, I *will* pee in the sink. The bathroom is at the end of a long, cold corridor and at this time is probably occupied. I unfold the flesh and take aim, swirling the yellow stream around the cracked porcelain bowl, catching and flushing down a hair which clings to the side. It lodges in the hole and winds itself around the latticework. I shake myself dry and then run the cold water, wiggling my forefinger to dislodge the hair.

A first glance in the mirror. It is so small and hung so low and so badly-lit that my morning face does not look as horrific as I'm sure it really is. Not at Craigbourne are to be found those cruel modern bathrooms with theatrical dressing-room bulbs dotted around the periphery of the glass, exposing every vein and pore and spot and line. I'm happy with the deception. I've lost that false confidence with which we build up some image of ourselves, some hope that in the right light on the right day at the right time we might awaken some sexual desire in the right person. I've let myself go, in body and in spirit. A beautiful man or woman

can still be beautiful in old age if they maintain an inner confidence and an erect posture. An upright spine and a bright eye
will compensate for a forest of wrinkles in the later years. I pull
yesterday's clothes over my sack of flab and head over to the
chapel to worship the God I don't think I've ever known.

15   MALAGA

I've been writing a lot on this retreat. 'Keep a journal', said the
bishop. 'Make notes.' A mandate to remember – not a fog of vague
thoughts, drifting mood-colours in the clouds, but grounded
words scratched, bleeding on to paper. Re-member. To piece
together the bits. To assemble once more the parts.

An autobiography? I wouldn't know how. There have not
been enough major events of interest in my life. But I've always
enjoyed the act of writing. I look forward to sitting at this desk
every day (I spend many, many hours here), searching for words
yet being sought by words too. Ideas as dialogue, an internal
conversation of discovery. My pen becomes a knife carving letters
into a tree's bark, yet the words themselves come back at me like a
scalpel cutting out a tumour – my soul's strange cancer.

So, here's the blade. I'm at Craigbourne this week because I
like sex. I like it a lot. I crave it. I spend money on it. Rent boys.
'Rent' isn't right though, that's like picking up a car from Hertz
for the weekend. 'Buy' is wrong too because there's no ownership
except the hour which passes between you. 'Pay' is closer, but cold.

Can you pay for an act so intimate that only someone working in a DNA laboratory could separate the intermingled sweat and semen pasted across your chests and between your thighs? A donation? Ah, too quaint, like the clink of change tipped into an Red Cross box. A gift? That's nicer but it suggests something spontaneous and extraneous which is not the case when you contact someone on a website and arrange to remove your clothes and his clothes and grind your bodies together until sated. No, there's no adequate term to describe this meeting-point of my need and his need. I have money, he wants money. I have a desire, he has a body which can satisfy that desire. Are we not both benefiting? Is there not a perfect complementarity here? Leased for a while, with no middleman. Gentleman's agreement: shake hands, shake dick.

And I am a fool. There is an equality of dependence – we both want each other, if in different ways, in that hour of nakedness – but the encounter is a lie. If I realized at the time that I was paying for an abstract sensation then that sensation would disappear. The only thing the boy wants from my trousers is the contents of my wallet. But for the encounter to work I have to put on an emotional mask and believe that if he doesn't find me sexy or exciting now that this could change any second. Suck in that stomach; yawn some colour into those cheeks; push your fingers through that thinning hair. Repulsion to attraction – how fickle the fuse! For me too. The excitement which flares to the madness of craving – erection straining every vein, heart spraining towards cardiac arrest – can disappear with one sarcastic, sibilant word, one large mole sprouting hair, one tooth missing, one gum-line of furred white plaque.

I know the most I can hope for is fondness from the boys, and professionalism, but my fantasies remain, and not just physical ones. The young ones who are my regulars, fully grown but not fully mature, I imagine guiding gently to wisdom. 'I have a reading list for you. I have tickets for the theatre. We're going on a trip to Paris, an afternoon in Oxford, a summer weekend in Norway. Oh, the fjords. We'll glide on a boat into the twilight and beyond, into the dark, water-rippling hours, your head in my lap, your eyes fixed on mine.'

Stupid illusion! Remember Ian? You took him on a weekend trip to Malaga but his eyes were on the boy standing at the bar. Do you remember? They exchanged glances, a lowering of the eyelids, a smile out of the corner of his lips, a too-slow sip of the bottle of Heineken. I tried to break the mood: 'Let's go for a walk in the old part of town, Ian. There's a beautiful Gothic church which looks so lovely at night-time.'

I could see him weighing it up. I could see he didn't want to join me. I could see him glance at the other boy again. I could see that he realized that I was paying for this holiday and for his flight home. I could see his resentment, then its calm, pragmatic replacement with resignation.

'Let's just have another drink here,' he said, lifting the lip of the beer bottle slowly, casually to his mouth, with another glance towards the boy at the bar.

'But there's a lovely pub near the church, Ian. We could get an ice cream too.' I could hear the whine in my voice, my stupid voice, my pathetic, old-man routine of ancient buildings and the romantic walk to find them, shaking out a crumpled map and moving the tip of my nose up and down to find the correct angle for my bifocals. And a bloody ice cream! Strangely I even sensed a trickling away of sexual energy along with my social impotence. I looked at him and suddenly felt a kind of revulsion. Why was I here? Why was I exposing myself to such humiliation, hiding in the half-light of dingy bars with my puffy face and wheedling smile? I knew my hair was greasy and thin (we'd walked up the hill and I was sweaty), and my eyes were tired, and my neck was like an old towel, and my ears full of sprouting hairs. I knew I was wearing an outfit which was slightly too small and slightly too young for me. Beige shorts over fat, sunburnt legs, a frontal hump under my new turquoise polo shirt. I felt a heave of sorrow.

'I'm going for a pee,' he said, standing up and walking past the bar with another heavy glance. It took four seconds for the boy to put down his wine glass, wipe his mouth, stand up, adjust his belt and saunter over in the same direction, to the men's room. He didn't even look at me, to register my jealousy. Perhaps he didn't even think about it, couldn't believe that we might be 'together'. I saw the door of the bathroom open for the second time before it was fully at rest from its first swinging. What could I do? Join them? Leave? No, I just sat there, looking at my drink, looking at my fingers holding on to the glass which contained the drink, my jaw slack and my back sore. It was more than three minutes before the boy appeared again and swivelled back into his seat at the bar to continue his drink. Maybe they had not spoken or communicated in any way. Maybe Ian had been taking a shit in a cubicle. Maybe they'd been blowing each other in a cubicle. Ian finally came out and walked back over to me, smiling.

'OK, let's go now. I'm kind of tired,' he said. Why did I know that somehow later the two of them would meet up and would batter against each other's bodies in frantic lust in some cheap room with rattling air-conditioning, clothes strewn on a dirty floor, clawing in passion until the final spray of ecstasy spilled over threadbare sheets?

I should return to prayer, I thought. I should take out my musty breviary, become pure, walk reverently up the cold marble steps to the altar, hands together, thumbs crossed, eyes down, lips kind but firm. I was resolved. A new path would not be that difficult to take. But then, the humid walk back to our hotel, cicadas chirping, washing hanging out of the windows, dogs licking at scraps in dark corners, a distant guitar strumming – Andalusia's hot breath. We arrived, then up to our room, then shoes off, then Ian plunged his tongue deep inside my ear. It was all I wanted.

I look back over my priesthood – twenty-five years, my anniversary is next year. How pointless it all seems, as if I had sailed to a desert island after my ordination and begun to live some weird fantasy life there about which no one knew anything or cared. My memories are like shells, dry and empty and dead, the tide creeping in and out and slowly reducing them to sand. Blank squares in a out-of-date diary.

What did I think my life would be after I was ordained? I'd lived around priests since infancy so I knew the public face, but I didn't know about the private failures and the sheer monotony of their lives. Failure: 'the omission of expected or required action', as one dictionary puts it. Interesting that it's defined as a passive fault... omission. Jobs have goals, the achievement of which is their very definition. To be a pilot is to fly a plane. To be a bricklayer is to lay bricks. Priesthood is infallibly 'effective', so the theologians tell us (we consecrate, forgive, bless, and it always works), but underneath theology's theoretical confidence is the constant undertow of practical failure. We fail to lift spirits or heal souls. We answer big questions with little lies. With a few exceptions (Father Damien with his lepers, Don Bosco with his urchins) we fail to make a difference, week after week. Omission is the invisible footprint behind every step.

Then there are fewer and fewer of us as every year passes. Countries where we sent missionaries in the 19th century now send missionaries to us. We have four foreign supply priests here in the Altrincham diocese, two from India, one from Brazil, and Father Chiwetel, the young, handsome Nigerian. They have tremendous energy but their enthusiasm is more dispiriting to me than contagious. It's too easy somehow. (Although with Father Chiwetel of course I was later to make an astonishing, disturbing discovery.)

And monotony. There are many monotonous jobs – workers on assembly lines or underground train drivers – but the priest lives with monotony of the soul. The liturgy's ring of words circling each day is made worse by the expectation that it should be uplifting or life-changing. This is a monotony which carries responsibility on weary shoulders. To say the same words every day. To walk out and say the same words, often to a gathering of three old women in a cold church. To dress up and light the candles and say the same words the same words the same words . . . and then not to believe them. Savour-less salt smarting in the cut.

My Silver Jubilee and my 50th birthday in the same year. Silver-haired jubilee, silver chest hair, silver pubic hair. Twenty-five years of half-mast, half-assed service. I've been sodomized at the very moment that a parishioner was gasping for a last breath in a hospice. I've gagged on the meat of a stranger's penis whilst my flock was being ravaged by wolves. I've joined the pack of wolves and buried my head deep into their tick-infested fur. Judas was paid thirty silver pieces for his betrayal. Five more to go . . .

The wounded healer appellation (from Jung, I think) is an attractive one for a priest. No priest is not a sinner. But there are times when the full extent of my moral decrepitude is suddenly made clear to me, as if I am handed a pair of strong binoculars and see with absolute horror of what my life truly consists. I'm terrified. It feels as if I wield an unsheathed knife, that I slash my way through my days, harming everything in my path – a wounder not a healer.

Occasionally when I'm travelling and the opportunity arises and I'm in the mood I will slip into a Confessional. Usually the priest is kind, brief and encouraging: 'Try to do better, Father' is about as far as it goes. But once on a trip to London I joined the queue at one of the bigger city churches. Finally it was my turn. I knelt in the shadows, and then the priest came at me like an enraged pit-bull terrier:

'Do you realize, Father, the damage you are doing living your priestly life as you are? The opportunities left unused, the graces cast aside, the hungry souls you could feed and to which instead you deny nourishment. Worse, you are contaminating the very food you are meant to distribute. You are a priest! Consecrated to God! And you're living like a spiritual slob. And having sexual encounters with all those people . . . what on earth do you think you're doing?'

'I don't know, Father. I . . .'

He interrupted, 'How many of these ... p-prostitutes have you paid for over the past year for instance?'

'I really can't say, Father. This week it's been two but ... '

'This week! You are a disgrace to the Church. A poisoner of souls. You need treatment. You need to undergo serious penance. Get yourself a regular spiritual director, Father. Have a plan of life. Say the rosary.' He sighed but not now with anger or irritability. I could tell he had begun to calm down.

'This isn't the time or place to go into this but phone me and we can arrange to meet outside and talk at greater length. You really do need help, Father. Anyway, for your penance I want you to ... ' He paused as if to think of something suitable. 'The rosary. Say all fifteen decades every day for the next month, on your knees, in front of the Blessed Sacrament. And now I absolve you of your sins in the name of the Father ... '

I agreed with his assessment in a way but the wrath, the impatience, the vexation in his voice, the sense that he had his life in order and therefore was able to help me sort out mine, destroyed any possibility of repentance for me. And, of course, he was the last person I would phone in a crisis. Maybe he was just tired that day – it can be exhausting sitting hour after hour in one of those airless boxes – but was he not also wielding an unsheathed knife? I've wounded people in my priestly life but so has he, in a different way, maybe worse. My lesions were legion but they were mostly superficial, scratches of passion, of weakness, of indulgence. He dug the blade deep. He was a surgeon without sutures.

Oh how I hated the rosary! I prayed five decades a day throughout my childhood and the ache of its monotony was a torture. The words seemed like metal in my mouth, the twenty minutes an endless yawn – no, not a yawn because I was wide-awake with exasperation. And on the rare occasions when I forgot: 'Have you said the rosary today, Joe?' Seeing my hesitation and my reluctance to lie about something so sacred, my mother would gently reprimand me: 'Could you not give even twenty minutes of your day to Our Lady? Never go to sleep without saying the rosary. It's your duty to our Blessed Mother. It makes her smile to see her children calling on her in this way.' I wasn't convinced but it was easier to do it than not. Out of bed I'd roll, on to my knees, the beads pulled one by one through my fingers. My not-so-blessed mother would smile and quietly leave the room. I'd finish the Litany of the Saints and imagine carving another notch on my bedpost of sanctity, another soul released from Purgatory's flames.

In the early years it felt good. A lot of traditional Catholic devotion is built on a kind of inoculation process: you make people sick with guilt, then supply the antidote; you inflict a wound and then, lo and behold, you have the magic ointment; you create a freezing room, watch people turn blue with theological hypo-thermia, and then turn on the heat. 'Your sins are forgiven. Go in peace.' And they do. Rosy cheeks warm. With a smile of joy. If a placebo cures the patient shouldn't the doctor be happy?

Then there were the public recitations of the rosary, after or before Mass. The little idiosyncrasies of each reciter: Blessed art thou *among* women or *amongst* women. Where to place the stresses or the pauses? And then those who would canter through the words in a blur, or begin the next 'Hail Mary' when we were still saying 'at the hour of our death, Amen'. I wanted to scream. When we reached the seventh bead I would feel a sense of relief: one more decade would soon be over.

Related to the rosary was the scapular. If you died wearing the brown scapular of Our Lady of Mount Carmel you would be released from Purgatory on the first Saturday after your death, the Sabbatine Privilege. My mother was never without her scapular and encouraged me to wear one too, a stringy thing with two brown patches worn like a yoke over the shoulders. It never stayed in place but rode up, tangling around the neckline in a semi-strangulation. The cloth became sweat-impregnated and dandruff-dusted so I used to wash mine once a week under the hot tap with a drop of shampoo. I knew I couldn't launder away its sacred properties but I was concerned that I might lose its benefits should I die when it was drying on the doorknob and not actually draped around my neck.

'Say the rosary, wear the scapular,' the constant message from the three children of Fatima to whom Mary had appeared in 1917. Interest in such apparitions was dying out by the time I entered the seminary, but my mother's generation was devoted to Lourdes and Knock and Loreto and especially to Fatima.

'Souls go to Hell because there is no one to pray for them,' said one of the seers. What can you reply to that except to get on your knees? Nothing wrong with prayer, but such an admonition so easily becomes a pathological source of obsession. It was for my mother. She awoke every morning to a cruel taskmaster, a God of calculations, a moneychanging tyrant who required her Hail Marys to persuade him to prevent souls from tumbling down to the abyss. She hadn't learned that any calculator God might have to measure our shortcomings perpetually resets to zero.

19   STRIPPED YOUTH

The terror of the morning. The brain's sudden brightness before the dawn. Bright with dark thoughts. Consciousness blindingly alert. Life's total irrelevance, its pinprick length a backdrop to the monstrous importance of every needlepoint moment. That sudden wake-up vision, sleep rubbed from eyes, the unavoidable face of the day. Is faith's bleakest black hole at this hour a clarifying (the magnifying mirror of grace) or a distortion of the truth? Is truth trees or the wood in which they grow? I turn over in bed, a rotting leaf in that forest, a lost child in that wilderness.

Lost childhood memories. The morning. Burrowed into bed. A shiver of delight. Safe in the tomb. Hideout. Scent of farts and hormones. I must not touch, mustn't even name it. I hear my mother downstairs. In the kitchen. She knows and sees everything. Holy purity. Sex. Outside of marriage not a thought not a word not a glance not a hint is permitted. St Francis rolled in the snow, another saint flung himself into a bramble bush, 'sticky as tar' said another. I feel my pyjamas stretch. I burrow deeper, darker. My pyjamas stiffen still further. Footsteps up the stairs. Door flung open. Bedclothes ripped aside, whimpering body, nowhere to hide, furious face glowering, slash of belt or palm's vicious smack. Downstairs toast is burning.

The winter day begins. The windows are caked with frost. I leap out of bed. To the cold bathroom. I can't pee until I lose my erection. The morning hard-on: Satan's salute. Frigid splash from the tap. Scooped-up to pat-down haystack hair. Unwashed dressing gown, grubby pockets, marmalade on sleeves. Three new pimples. Acne's spots on top of earlier scars. Squeeze to red blotch. Pimples still unexploded. Pick nose clean of night's mucus. Twist arms through creased school uniform. Yesterday's shirt's filthy collar. Slurp Nescafé from a beige mug. Freezing milk bottle's condensation. Butter-smeared knife in the slosh of cold, unsoapy water. Unfinished homework. Undigested breakfast. Cramp of constipation. Greasy hair still sticking up. Satchel on shoulder then dash to school.

How clearly I remember those cruel, youthful mornings, the mood of which seems destined to repeat like clockwork up to the wind-down of life's final, futile evening: coals to clinkers to dust in the slumbering, ashen grate.

When my mother began to lose her memory I began to lose my inhibitions. Her decline was steep and I followed her down the slope. I was at her house one afternoon when I realized in the course of our conversation that nothing I said was registering, everything was slipping through the fingers of her mind, her attention was completely unfocused. She said some wildly irrational things during my visit and twice lashed out with bizarre, vicious remarks. For the whole of my life until that moment it was as if she had been standing next to me, watching everything I did. Now, as her mind began to soften, I felt like she was out of the room, out of earshot. It was disturbing and liberating in equal measure.

The back pages of a free newspaper picked up by chance in the dentist's office: 'Manchester City Centre, M4M, 23, sensual massage, student', along with a phone number. It wasn't the first time I'd been tempted to try some casual sexual activity, but my sense of disorientation after my mother's deterioration opened a door for me. In losing her grip on herself she was losing her grip on me. I suddenly felt reckless. Massage? Why not! My shoulders were tight. It was sensual not erotic, probably just physical therapy really. An unregistered osteopath. I didn't need to do more than I felt comfortable doing. I wonder what he looks like? My heart began racing.

I phoned. He answered. We spoke for just seconds and made an appointment for the following evening. Instantly I began to tremble in anticipation and I wondered how I would manage to wait for twenty-four hours. It became the whole focus of my mind. When he opened his door I saw that he was quite handsome and I was nervous as I undressed down to my underpants and lay down on my stomach on the bed. It was all fairly innocent and he was not especially competent. He remained dressed in baggy sweatpants and a hoodie throughout and eventually asked if I'd like to remove my underwear. I did so as he turned me over and then the massage turned more sensual as he touched my genitals and the kneading strokes became longer and more teasing. It didn't take much for me to have an orgasm and he reached for a conveniently nearby roll of toilet paper to clean me up.

It would be hard to call it having sex as his involvement was so completely detached, without the slightest hint that he might have been interested or excited. He might just as well have been wiping a saucepan clean in the sink as removing semen from my stomach. His jerking me off was more like milking a cow than making love: an udder was full, it needed someone to empty it. My physical relief was palpable but inside I felt empty and down-cast. He had performed a service for me but it felt like I was the one being used, tossed into the toilet bowl like the soggy tissue paper he was holding in his hands.

It was a few weeks before I decided to try another one. This guy was much more skilful and when I began to get aroused he offered some extra services for extra cash. As he took off his clothes and then lay on top of me I could tell that my initial curiosity could easily turn into an addiction. Nothing had ever excited me like this. Everything else in my life seemed drab in comparison. Soon it became a routine: a visit to see my declining mother, then intimacy in a bedsit with a young man. 'Do you offer any extra services?' I would ask, with increasing boldness. Eventually I only used websites where extra was not extra. I always carried a condom in my trousers. Left pocket. Next to my rosary.

21   MY LATE MOTHER

Alzheimer's got her early. Mother drooling in the armchair at the nursing home, always mumbling. Fidgeting and mumbling. The transition from a sharp mind to a shattered memory was quick and cruel. For her. For me.

Mumbling then a screech, a demented canary's cry. She was as thin as a canary by this point. Her features had sharpened, her cheeks sunken, her nose a blade-beak between vacant, hollow eyes. She would gape passively past everything with plasticine eyes and then suddenly a wild stare would spring out of her head, and a cackle – a jack-in-the-box of fearsome, malevolent energy.

The fire in the kitchen (she had been making cheese on toast) was the final straw, when I realized that she could no longer live on her own, that she needed to be taken care of in a specialized environment. It was a terrible day when I drove her to the nursing home. I told her it was just for a couple of weeks, like a holiday; a small hotel in the country, I said. I think both of us knew that the other knew that the other knew . . . but she didn't kick up a fuss. We drove up to the front and I took out her little tartan suitcase from the boot.

Had she not been pregnant with me when my father died I think she would have become a nun in the aftermath of that tragedy. Now, in her own declining years, she was to live in a home run by nuns. Perhaps she could make-believe she was finally a member of a religious order. She seemed to improve in her first months there, she was more relaxed and, ironically, less religiously obsessed. A steep change from my earlier memories of her when everything was surrounded with prayers – note, I don't say prayer. The piling up of ejaculations (yes, that's what they were called in more innocent times), short phrases spoken under the breath: 'Jesus mercy, Mary help', 'Into your hands I commend my spirit', 'Oh Sacred Heart, I trust in thee'. A simple, unregulated way to pray until the Church added indulgences to the practice and anxious souls like my mother found themselves tallying up the numbers. If simply saying 'Jesus, Mary and Joseph' gained an indulgence of a hundred days applicable to the Holy Souls in Purgatory then saying it five times . . . well, you get my drift. It was impossible not to become entangled in a web of scrupulosity, and I don't think there was a minute in the day when she was not filling her spiritual basket with such trinkets.

But when she entered the nursing home a lot of this began to melt away. The nuns grew to love her and she found a peace of soul I don't think she'd ever had before. Then eventually the inevitable happened. She ceased to tread the water of mere memory loss and began to sink underneath the waters of dementia, her personality floating away, drifting out to sea. I visited three or four times a week and would sit with her for hours just holding her hand, helpless, waiting for a smile of recognition, something I could hold on to. Then one morning I got a call from one of the nuns to tell me that she was unconscious. I couldn't help wonder what she meant by 'unconscious'. Had my mother not been so for the best part of a year now, unaware of people, events, herself? I knew this might be the end so I rushed over to give her the Last Rites.

I looked down at that heap of bones and it filled me with horror. We'd been too claustrophobically close throughout my life for us to have any healthy love for each other, but now a new horror surfaced. I was terrified at the sheer joy I was feeling. I was actually bubbling over with jubilation at the impending freedom, not hers but mine. I had done everything in my life for her approval and I almost certainly became a priest to receive her final, supreme endorsement. I write this now with bitterness. Not so much because I became a priest but because I allowed such blackmail to shape my life. And my resentment at her years of control over me meant that I couldn't be the sort of support for her at the end of her life that I should have been. She represented oppression for me. Everything had had conditions and had been done under a kind of moral duress. I looked at this dying woman hoping (God forgive me!) that she wouldn't recover.

I anointed her and sat staring at her vacant face. A helpless baby in a nursery, a helpless woman in a nursing home. Life's mad circle. A beginning and an end in slobber and slime, and, in between, the noontide slobber and slime of food and soap and snot and sex. Life's span a trash can into which leftovers are scraped. She died the next day, and after her funeral I put her few possessions – some books and photos and clothes and the tartan suitcase – into two black bin bags. Now all that is left are these words, these bitter memories... until my own powers fail.

22 INFANTILISM

There were times during the years my mother was in the nursing home when I felt as if I never spoke to an adult. With her it was all baby talk and nonsense, then in the schools I visited: 'Good morning, boys and girls.' 'Good morning, Father.' And in church the daily Mass: 'The Lord be with you – And also with you – And also with you – And also with you.' The liturgy's ping-pong greeting. Then the sermons I preach every Sunday but which I don't believe. 'God is telling us that ...' No, he isn't! 'God cares about every one of you ...' No, he doesn't! Endless childish excuses and fairy tales. Futile babble. Only in an escort's bedroom do I feel grown up and alive, apron strings finally slashed loose, the straw of blather burnt away by the fire of body's blush and follicles' rising. 'Adults Only' on my computer screen takes on a whole new meaning in my kindergarten life.

Yet adults? Grown-ups? We who are mere ants crawling on a planet the size of an ant's toenail. Our clever thoughts, our fragile emotions a mere nose-hair of importance in the Milky Way. 'And also with you...and also with you', the naivety of the exchange. Yet isn't it that basic human connection which I seek every time I get into my car and drive to a rent boy's bedsit? And also with you, next to you, inside you. My 'maturity' drives me to solitude but it is the children, the young at heart, who are having all the fun. They are having a huge party to which I refuse the invitation. And whilst they shriek with delight I sit alone in silence, time sucked away, body dried up, libido an increasingly irrelevant page fading and crumbling with each turn.

23   LONELINESS

I feel terribly lonely a lot of the time but I'm ashamed and embarrassed to admit it. It suggests that no one wants to spend time with me, that I am a social failure. People talk about the loneliness of a priest, as if those who are not married are necessarily lonely. Sex has little to do with it, companionship more, but the worst is the sudden change from full church to empty house. That hurts the most. Closing the main doors after the Sunday evening Mass and watching families pile into cars. Locking those big doors, those silly, heavy, medieval doors with their giant latch like something out of *Alice in Wonderland*. Then tidying up. The hymn books, the Mass sheets, the newsletters, candles, cruets, linens, chalices, patens…liturgy's theatre, its doll's house, its playpen, its sandpit. And then the switching off of lights. If I had one big master switch it would be less sad, but there are six small brown buttons at Sacred Heart, each one blinking out a set of lights, six ghostly antiphonal choirs reduced to silence.

I have an address book. I have twenty, twenty-five people I could always phone and invite over for dinner if I wanted to. Some kind parishioners, some kind priests. But religion. We'd talk about religion and the liturgy and the parish pilgrimage to Walsingham and the Day of Prayer for Vocations and the youth group and the readers' rota. Then this time of the year there's the Nativity play. The incessant fuss about costumes and who will play Joseph or the Three Wise Men. 'Do you remember when Lucy was the Virgin Mary and she knocked over the cow? Her face was a picture!' 'Have you ordered the Christmas tree? Best to get it early, just in case.' 'I think the fairy lights from last year have broken. We should get a new set. Morrisons have a special offer this weekend if you spend more than £20.' 'Another coffee?' 'Oh no, we really must be going. It's getting late.' A quick look at their watches with fake surprise. 'Goodness, how time flies.'

On other evenings there are official visitors like the engaged couples who come for marriage preparation. I'm in my study. The doorbell rings. I answer it. It's John and Mary. 'Hello, welcome. Come in. Would you like a coffee?' Love in their eyes. She's keen. He's a little embarrassed. Not thought much about religion. Shifts in his chair. Looks at the bookshelf. Children. Patience. Humour. Sacrament. Forgiveness. Tolerance. Condoms? No. Pills? No. Try natural methods. Billings. Ovulation. They smile at each other. I smile at them. Energy as he stands up. Sexy. He can't wait to leave. Out the door. Goodbye. See you next week. Engine starts. Car revs. They drive off. I close the door and suddenly feel desperately sad.

It's not so much that I want to be in their place, although such youthfulness and naturalness are cruelly attractive in my state of bitterness. No, I feel sad because it was a wasted opportunity. I wanted to help them in some way, to help them to see more clearly that marriage is a sacrament where they can meet Christ in every act of their nuptial life, in the bedroom of course but also in the kitchen and on holiday, in sickness and in health, Christ blessing them in the ordinary things over the ordinary years. My heart wells up as I sit there after they leave. The priest should be a channel of grace, a conduit flowing with blessings, a light sensor in every room. But I stiffen when faced with situations of flesh and blood. My heart closes with a reflex. I become a hardback book, riddled with theories as if with worms, a whole bookcase of hardback books, brittle and musty. I take the dirty coffee cups into the cold kitchen and rinse them under the cold tap, the squirt of detergent (too much) a translucent green gob on top of the brown stains.

But there is Christopher, my old friend from school, and his three lovely kids. I do enjoy going over to their house. He and

Ann are gracious and fun. But still I feel I can't be myself, even there. I can't unbutton the black shirt under which weep incurable, unmentionable wounds. My religious autopilot works but I long to find that ease, that openness on which friendship thrives. Should I wait for people to reach out to me or do I need to reach out to them first? What does it mean to have a friend? Why does one person want to spend time with another? Do I have enough funny stories to keep the conversation afloat? Did I already tell that joke last time? They're laughing. Is it still amusing or are they just being polite? Am I speaking too much? Am I speaking too little?

One way I avoid thinking about my loneliness is to visit the sick in hospital. I go three times a week. It gets around. My parishioners are impressed. But I don't go there to put on a show, rather to fill the isolated hours, to do something, to cover up something. To bargain with God. A wager, that's it! To stack some chips on the mottled green felt, to pile them high enough so they hide me as I slump against the table, to push a few of them on to the fading squares as the croupier watches and waits: red or black, odd or even, safer bets even if God's zero is always weighed in his favour. The wheel spins. The small white ball spits in the bouncing grooves. I walk away. I don't care. The chips come and go and win and lose. They're all scooped up when switched-on lights fake the dawn.

I have abused my vow of celibacy with a certain recklessness.
I'm not proud of it but I'm tired and battered and I haven't the
energy to be ashamed. Yes, I've mined deep in the pit of sexual
gratification, in recent years as often and as greedily as I could –
fingers pressed to the bottom of the mud pool. But I'm not alone
amongst priests. Many of my brethren 'indulge' a little. Some,
once a year, take off for a fortnight in Ibiza or to a Greek island
and lose their hearts to a Juan or a Nikos, amnesia under the sun
or in the cool of the cheap hotel, forgiveness safely awaiting them
in the Confessional before their budget flight home. It is enough.
A fervent spurt from the tap then a new rubber seal until the
following season; a deciduous relief; Easter's yearly rising to new
life; the fat candle extinguished but a book of matches waiting
safely in the drawer.

And then there are those priests, seemingly pure, whose
minds reek of the stale perfume of boy-obsession. The altar
server's floppy blond hair falling over his grubby surplice, his
voice breaking, spots appearing, the down on lip and chin and
cheek, the shirt hanging loose outside the roughed-up trousers, a
faint smell of sweat and the mist of acrid breath: the beautiful need
not bathe; those with a heavenly smile have no need of toothpaste.
Never a finger laid, no touching, never a brush with flesh, but
eyes . . . devouring deep-down. As if embracing into form the
adolescent's body with a sculptor's virtual hands, or as a potter's

slop and spin caresses the slippery clay into a sphere. A longing gaze, or more often a surreptitious glance, roaming up and down, and there's the flash of stomach, oh look away, then look back and up to the face and the lips (let me kiss away that speck of spittle) and then a peek inside the smooth curve of the neckline where three moles lead down towards the ridge of the spine and … stop!

These priests would have *those* books on their coffee tables, Housman or Firbank, a biography of Oscar Wilde or Bosie ('both became Catholics, you know') or the other sodomite converts, Brideshead's slim-chested band of brothers. A taste for classical music too, and opera, always opera. Piles of CDs, the open mouths of Maria, Joan, Cecilia, Renée in tottering stacks of plastic cases, costumed from Meyerbeer to Puccini. Admittance to actual performances was expensive but friendships (nodding, winking) with cultured parishioners would often procure one free ticket. But even without the comps, for the price of my wank in Wythenshawe Father X could be sitting in ecstasy on a crimson velvet seat, perched up in the gods at the opera house, programme book crinkled with perspiring palms, just waiting, waiting for that high C to hit his diva G-spot.

25   SAVED

Believe! What? How?

Evangelicals talk about it with ease and with a flourish: a one-off decision to accept Christ as your 'personal saviour'

(6:06PM on the 14th of September 1980) is a ticket without an expiration date to the banquet which never ends. You don't even have to hold on to the warranty because it's kept safe on Heaven's central database – although the niggling question always remains: did I *really* make the choice? Was the form filled out correctly? For strict Calvinists it's even simpler. The moment the father's sperm and the mother's ovum unite and a human being is created it is predestined to eternal life...or not.

Catholics have a saner and more scriptural understanding of such soteriological matters. Every individual has a choice which remains active up to the moment of death. The only problem is that this choice can be negative as well as positive – and what are we choosing anyway? We can merely choose to avoid mortal sin, but is that enough? What about sins of omission? They're literally limitless.

Monsignor Ronald Knox and Sir Arnold Lunn published a book-length discussion which included the hypothetical case of a man who died in an accident one Sunday when deliberately choosing a game of golf over Mass, which would be a mortal sin. Did he go straight to Hell? Knox, a good man, wriggled around the plain teaching as best he could and his apologetic squirming on the page suggested that he would have substituted himself for the golfer rather than allow the teaching to take effect – truly a Christ-like response. But to undo the curse of eternal damnation was surely the whole point of Christ's coming to earth in the first place. If we are merely left with some obscure instructions for the lottery by which we might be able to avoid the curse, what is the good of that? Only the cancellation of the curse is Good News.

Maybe the Calvinists are right: the decision is made at conception – except that no one can be lost. Every sperm joins every ovum in a graceful linking of arms; the kick of every foetus in every womb is a dance of joy.

26 NIJINSKY

I rarely meet someone for sex without money changing hands. I prefer it because it means I have control over when it happens (and finishes), and it means that I don't have to please the boys. I can come and go as I wish without their approval. Any healthy relationship is based on a certain sort of equality (ergo the Greeks' man-boy love never impressed me as a model for today), but I don't want a relationship. It would be too fixed. It would mean 'living in sin'. My preferred method is to sin and then to begin again after a good Confession – a house in the country to be opened up then locked up at will, not a permanent home. A boyfriend would make this equivocation impossible. Now I can leave the Confessional and return home to my microwaved supper with an easy conscience. Not so if I were to arrive at my front door to the smell of supper already cooking on the stove and the sight of my slippers warming by the fire. Moreover, my sexual energy is scatter-gunned. I'm excited by a man's hands exploring my naked body, but I'm more excited by a constant variety of hands. 'Oh, for a thousand tongues!' I want to taste a thousand kisses on my lips, to feel ten thousand teeth biting into my neck.

But more than all of that, when I'm paying I can create the perfect make-believe world. I know my escort will want to try to please me, often saying flattering things and pretending to be aroused (the best ones are so good at it) because then he'll get a bigger tip. And surrounded by his honeyed words and fake groans of ecstasy I can happily live out my sexual fantasies. And then I can switch them off. My finger always on the button. I'm wearing the trousers, even when (temporarily) I'm not. I can fool myself that it is a service like visiting the barber's shop: short back and sides, touch me there, stop doing that, do that some more. I have the menu in front of me and I can order exactly what I want, pay for it, then leave.

I did try a couple of the new smartphone apps which miraculously display gay men on the screen arranged by distance: Jerry is 200 metres away, and there is a photo of (one has to trust) Jerry, flexing his biceps in a gym somewhere. 'Ready for action' his profile states. Man after man, endlessly pouting chests, puckered lips, sly, seductive eyes, peacock feathers splayed, mating calls a silent cacophony from listing to listing – bottom, top, versatile, vanilla, no strings, no attachments, straight-acting, stay cool, walk away, discreet, blocked. I was curious at first but reached a dead end when filling out my profile. I reduced my age by ten years and my weight by twenty kilos (I could always go on a diet), but I couldn't say anything about myself or what I was looking for which sounded plausible. And then to upload a photo. Not only was I scared to have pictures of my face or other body parts flashing into public view on people's phones but I have enough self-knowledge to know that money is my greatest asset with handsome young men.

I have a paunch, ugly legs and a small penis – not the words to use as meat magnets on Craigslist or Grindr. I tried taking a few shots of my naked chest one reckless afternoon. God, was my flesh *really* that colour, and so pasty and puffed? I didn't need to cover up my groin, my stomach does that for me.

On one of the apps I ended up posting a photo of Nijinsky reclining as the Faun for my profile, thinking the reference would pique the curiosity of the sort of men I might want to meet. The interesting ones wanted a date which I then realized I couldn't pursue after all, and the stupid ones thought it was really me: 'Hey, do you have another pic, without the loincloth?' 'Great legs, dude.' Then I realized, because the Cruisadaddy app is for young men who like older men (and the, oh so common, reverse), that I was getting all the oldies. Beautiful young guys in this community were turned on by white chest hair and dried-up nipples. I should have uploaded a picture of Diaghilev. 'Daddies' – the irony of the paternal nomenclature was not wasted on this ageing priest.

Public toilets? Well, a couple of times I looked over at a handsome face and then looked down to the stream of steaming urine and its source, but the smell, and the damp, dank floors, and the buzz of the flies, and the possibility of arrest, and the sheer visibility of it all makes me uneasy. Once I was sitting in a cubicle at a men's department store and a note appeared under the divider: 'wanna suck me off?' I ignored it and left hurriedly, but outside I decided to wait to see from whom the offer had come. I stood there amidst the rows of suits and trousers and ties for a good ten minutes and then shuffling out slowly in an old tweed coat too big for him came a scrawny man with a few wisps of white hair and badly-fitting false teeth. His gait had something of infinite sadness about it, as if each step was a pulling down as well as a pulling forward, a slouching towards the grave. He carried an old plastic carrier bag with a free local newspaper sticking out of it and there was a plastic triangle of sandwiches bulging along one side. I followed him out into the street and was on the point of inviting him, out of pity, to join me for a cup of coffee – but then I walked away.

27   KINDNESS

Some people seem to have a physical aptitude for kindness, a certain look in the eye or turn of the mouth, not so much a smile as a softening of features, a giving way without giving in. They invite you into their space without insisting you give up your space. They simply create a neutral area of acceptance. It's a gift. Bishop Bernard has it. It's not a question of an excessive friendliness – he is not a pal to his priests; no, his distance from them enables them to trust him more, beyond feelings or favourites. He knows that sometimes to say nothing, with a kind countenance and an open heart, can be to express everything.

I actually don't know how Bernard was promoted to the episcopacy in the first place. He has no regal bearing, no smooth public face, no dazzling double degrees, and he has never worked in Rome, which is a frequent fast-track to mitre and ring. Everything about him is normal, modest, hidden. Yes, he ran his previous parishes effectively and energetically but nothing exceptional appeared to be happening as far as an outsider could see. Nevertheless there was a significant increase of communicants wherever he went, and charitable works seemed to sprout up spontaneously.

Cheerfulness can be the opposite of kindness when it exists in a form which suggests superiority. Father Neville's relentless bright eye staring at me every morning above his cold-water smile is a perfect example of this. His bright optimism is a shiny platinum membership card to an exclusive club from which I'm excluded. And once I'd shared with him something of my sexual addiction, even without details, there was no going back. I'd lost the virginity of my propriety, that badge of Catholic honour for the celibates who hold the reins of power in the Church. Only eunuchs may wear the crowns. A body sticky with the sap of life is disqualified. Blackballed.

But my faith, tattered as it is, still has threads strong enough to withstand Father Neville's smugness. He lacks authenticity. I can laugh at him. And in a way his priggishness is easier to side-step than my bishop's kindness. I am safer in my unrepentance with Neville. I can remain sitting in my pool of sin, mud lapping against my leg, brown-splashed past knees to loins. Its stench keeps others at bay. I don't want to change. But Bishop Bernard's compassion reminds me that I've become hardened, that my ground is so dry and barren that water just rolls away, that the effort involved in turning my life around would be more than I could bear.

28 BEDSITS

A rent boy's bedsit – a rabbit hutch in which to sleep and study and eat and defecate and fuck, paying off student loans one dirty old man at a time.

Poverty need not be squalor but with these flats it usually was. Victorian villas divided up with indecent, post-war haste, old curtains sagging behind filthy windows. One step on to the drafty porch where a dozen doorbells spew tangled wires out of a rough board of buttons. Faded, transient names on mailboxes containing only bills and junk, creased envelopes sullenly wedged inside the rusting apertures.

Inside the flats there are leaks which seep with acrid water, every crack forming yet more cracks. Condensation dribbling down into mould, then mushrooming into more mould – bunions of mildew at the base of the rotting sills. Cardboard walls and inherited carpets which push up to cobwebbed skirting boards with a rind of detritus.

The cooking arrangements were always nauseating. A sauce-scarred pan resting on a cold hot-plate. Dishes jumbled in the sink. Moral disarray mirrored in domestic neglect. Filthy kitchen, filthy bedroom; food and sex. The nauseous symmetry of these two natural appetites of human survival melted down to lard: a candy bar for a diabetic.

Without the intoxication of lust I might well have retched at some of the beds I sank into. The odorous cocktail on a prostitute's sheets – oil, sweat, sperm, cheap aftershave. Under the blankets the faded but still-clear stains from last week's weak wash. There too the stray pubic hair's squiggle and the metallic wrapping hastily ripped then discarded from an earlier condom. The scrunched-up sheets, the flabby mattress – no monk's pallet or yogi's futon here. But don't get too comfortable in your horizontal recline on the coiled divan because once you've ejaculated, wiped off and paid the piper you're outta there. Past the encrusted pan through the cardboard door in the cardboard wall down the narrow staircase past the tangle of wires hanging from the doorbells into the cold, unforgiving night. The contemptuous night. No, don't dramatize . . . rather the oblivious night. Catch the night's eye if you can. But you can't. It looks past you. The best it can do is to hide you between the yellow lampposts as you limp along in your damp underpants – crotch sticky, testicles milked dry – along your path of unrepose.

When you speak to no one all day long (except Father Neville) and have no distractions, meal times become like sugar-water to a laboratory rat. Around four o'clock I start looking forward to dinner. I watch the clock, willing it forward.

It was the old monastic tradition for one of the community to read aloud during mealtimes but this practice has been replaced at Craigbourne by audio books – extracts from spiritual writers read by actors. This week we have sermons of St Augustine, whose relentless energy serves to make me more listless than ever. Simon Callow's magnificent voice relishes the melodious, archaic contours of the language whilst, I imagine, keeping the actual message of the 'theologian of the West' at arm's length. He (Simon) has become my friend this week, a strange comfort in the midst of my desolation. I listen to the music of the words without caring about their meaning. They are a *vocalise* resonating through the prison bars, stealing me away from Craigbourne and carrying me off to some garden of delights.

I see Father Neville praying into his food, head down, back straight, starving himself of pleasure despite the necessity of nutrition. What if he were to relish the flavours? Wouldn't that be more holy? To eat a tomato with mindfulness requires detachment, allowing time for it to reveal its delights, waiting, contemplating, with patience, with reverence, with gratefulness.

Without gratefulness life is pale and tuneless, a piano without hammers, a Stradivarius without strings. 'Now what do you say?' my mother used to say to me, the little boy in the short trousers. 'Thank you, Mrs Armitage,' I would lisp. My mother knew that such gratitude would eventually mean more to me than to the one who had given me the lemon drizzle cake that Saturday afternoon.

30   RONNIE

Ronald Knox spoke about insomnia's dark hour. It's four o'clock in the morning and you're lying in bed, wide awake, wider awake than during daytime. Awake to the emptiness of it all, the failure of it all, the futility of it all. No one wants a friend who phones at four o'clock in the morning. Kettles don't whistle so early, toast is not buttered or burned at that ungodly hour. It is dark outside the curtains, cold inside the curtains – the sheets shroud a restless cadaver.

Well, he didn't quite put it like that, but we can read between the lines. This eccentric priest, shining like a jewel then chiselled out of the ring, replaced by glass. Given a life's task then, at the point of handing it over, every facet perfectly, brilliantly shaped . . . all thrown away. He slaved on a translation of the Bible, from the Latin. Only the Latin is authentic. Finish it, Ronnie, and we'll use it in the Mass. Your luminous words will inspire souls from Timbuktu to Toledo.

He poured his heart into it, wishing he could use the Greek which he knew as well as St Jerome's Vulgate. He allowed himself a few footnotes, a few caveats. No Ronnie, the Latin. Don't be obstinate. Don't be disobedient. Don't be like your heretic father, the Anglican Archbishop. Language of the Church, if you don't mind. Language of the Liturgy, if you please. Sacred language. You know we're going to have the readings in the vernacular soon. So people can understand. We want a fresh, accurate translation. Every word. We trust you, Ronnie. We're relying on you, Ronnie. Things are changing. Just think, Ronnie. From Toledo to Timbuktu.

But then, ink still wet on the page, things moved in a different direction and they decided to use a translation from the Greek after all. Ronnie's four o'clock in the morning sweats, his headache-inducing days squinting over texts, his typewriter's pitter-patter . . . all thrown away. A dead letter as he handed over his life's work. Ah well, all for the glory of God. Offer it up, Ronnie. Offer it up, for the good of souls. For the Holy Souls. A day of Purgatory erased for every word typed. One of the Church's most brilliant intellects forced to take refuge in eccentricity and pipe tobacco. There's a lot you can hide under a baggy tweed jacket behind a cloud of St Bruno. His subtle mind, a scalpel, was forced to hack like a lumberjack. Blunt blade, badly cut wood. Offer it up, Ronnie.

Unlike Ronald Knox I usually sleep well. It's my sanity. It's ten o'clock in the morning when I face my darkest hours on this retreat. Father Neville breezes in at 9:30 and talks at me, asks what I've been praying about, then breezes out. Another soul brought closer to our Blessed Lady. Finger the beads. Touch the scapular. Ouch, that cilice is sharp. Stone in the shoe. Every step a step closer to sanctity. *Deo gratias!*

Then it's ten o'clock. About ten minutes after he leaves. It's silent in my room. It's raining outside. I feel like shit. The day opens like an empty coffin, nothing inside, not even a velvet lining. I can't pray I can't read I can't think. Ah, but I can masturbate. And I do, lying on the bed, imagining the most terrible things being done to me. I masturbate. And writing this down now, later the same day, makes me want to write the M word a thousand times. I want to say to Father Neville tomorrow when he asks about the progress of my prayer: 'Father, I lay down on that bed over there, see it? Look!' I want to point and force him to turn his stiff, starched neck in his high, white collar. I want to watch his face crumple with blanched horror: 'There!' I'm shouting now and others outside can hear me. 'There!' I'm pointing at the bed. 'There! I masturbated yesterday, pulling up and down, up and down, up and down.' My hand curls in the air, faking the act in his face. He is looking at me in speechless disgust. 'And it felt good. It felt very good.'

A fifteen year old comes to me: 'Father, can I talk to you? The thing is, I'm gay.' What can I say? I have two options within the teaching of the Church: 'It's an intrinsic disorder and you must be celibate for the rest of your life'; or: 'There are treatments for this. Let me find a summer camp where they can cure you of your unnatural desires.' Actually what I end up saying is something along the lines of being gay being a gift from God. A different path. An example of the fascinating, complex variety of human life. One of Hopkins's 'dappled things'. I believe this, even if I've not lived it. I see it as my weakness rather than my hypocrisy. And my time slot in history. When I was born it was still 'the love that dare not speak its name', but the world has changed. And today's teenager dares to speak its name.

In some ways it was easier to be a pastor in Bosie's day. The young person in question would not have had the courage to come to me openly in the first place, nor would he have had the word to describe what he knew himself to be. So he would have remained in the closet, made it cosy, closed its door to affection, companionship and intimacy. The lucky ones became eccentric bachelors, academics, hardworking oddballs, favourite uncles. Then there were those whose eccentricity blurred into madness, whose hard work became obsession and insomnia, whose solitude became searing loneliness, whose sadness sliced sharply to suicide. Others became priests, in some ways the best option.

Being 'Father' instantly silences any probing questions about a future family: 'Have you got a girlfriend? When are you getting married? You're not...one of *those* are you?' The priesthood supplies the most elegant evasion, a place in a community of like-minded brethren, the promise of a front seat in Heaven, and, in case that's not enough, all topped off with the cherry of a free car and a housekeeper. What's not to like?

What's not to like is the cauldron of deception, the pink lips puckering easy blessings, the fire of lust subsumed into custard tarts. If only one bishop would come out with it: 'I'm gay and celibate.' Is there not one role model out there? These leaders demand continence for life from the fifteen year old, but cannot offer a finger of support, of empathy, of humility, of taking the risk that they might appear a little less than perfect. 'But you, my son, embarking on life's journey, just abstain. With the help of grace and our Blessed Mother all will be well. It will be hard at times, but trust in God. I know you wake up at night in a sweat of desire, your heart pumping, your cock about to explode. Reach for the rosary! Offer it up!' I'm afraid that's not enough, you gay, celibate, pink-faced, tart-devouring bishops. The choice you give us is either to behave like good sons of the Church and feather the nest of our closet or to leave the closet and the Church. You're buggered if you do and buggered if you don't.

But then I look in the mirror. And laugh bitterly. I'm not afraid to admit (privately) to being gay but I can't tell the teen-ager I'm happy or celibate. In five years I may be phoning him for his sexual services: '20, VGL, hung, versatile . . .' the honeyed words of seduction for predator bees like myself. Sucking deep, dying with the sting, and then like a scrawny alley cat back for nine lives more.

33   FRED ASTAIRE

Prostitution can be an easy way for a young person to make money. A wad of tax-free cash in hand without leaving the bedroom except to let in the punter. The best ones make you believe that they are attracted to you. They tip you over the edge to climax whilst either pretending to join you or sidestepping the moment like some Fred Astaire, leaving room for another dance later the same evening. They pretend that they find your flabby body sexy and the hairs sprouting out of your nose and ears endearing. They learn the technique of exhaling when kissing to avoid the retch of bad breath, or they manage to avoid kissing altogether. Speed is of the essence because most men, after reaching an orgasm, want to leave the scene of the crime quickly. An hour-long appointment can be cut short after fifteen minutes if climax is accomplished. The man with a premature ejaculation is a hooker's delight – the engine of his car outside still warm, libido's fast-food fix.

Many of the boys I see are students, textbooks laid to one side ready to be picked up again after pocketing the pound notes. An hour on the sweaty bed and calculus or chemistry or graphic design can be resumed with little effort. Not so the students who slave in the kitchens of dingy restaurants, arriving home exhausted after midnight on minimum wage or less. I feel that even if my boys are not enjoying it they are benefiting from it. I am the kind old uncle helping with the tuition fees, even if it pains me to think of myself as old in that situation.

How desperate it all is. How pathetic I know myself to be as I climb back into my car and drive home smelling of their cologne and their drying sweat and sometimes with even a whiff of faecal matter. I am in a state of constant denial, excuses on top of excuses, hands over eyes, torn in every direction, self-pitying and self-condemning in one desperate cry. I am the judge, the prosecution and the defence in a shambolic, tawdry equivocation. My soul is dead, a cheap cigarette butt ground to dust with a heavy heel.

34   TENDERNESS

But just occasionally, in the post-coital cooling down, spent and lying in suspended time, I am overcome by a moment of tenderness. His finger traced down my arm, a sideways glance, a coy smile, something beyond the mere financial transaction, beyond stuffing when starving at a feast. The calm consolation of human contact. Lust's fierce battle cry (the blaze of guns, the screech of bullets) finally quietened for a moment. A truce. It might only be for seconds, a mere mote on the lens, but there sometimes takes place a gentle sharing of vulnerability. Then a slow, reluctant getting off the bed, standing, stretching, resentful at the passing of time, at the loosening of the embrace. Another slow glance. Another slow smile. But then, the slow reaching for my wallet.

'No. I don't want paying this time,' he says, leaning over and touching my arm affectionately. 'What we shared was so special. It's never been like that with anyone else. I really like you, you know . . . do you want to stay overnight? I want to wake up in your embrace, our legs entwined, our bodies joined together.' He takes hold of me in his strong arms and lowers me gently back on to the bed and begins to give me a massage, long strokes, caressing gestures. Ha! In my dreams. However tender the boys seem it is always an act. Some of them are Oliviers of the mattress but the money always leaves my pocket and enters theirs. Our period of intimacy is measured as if an egg timer were trickling dust through the sphincter of its glass bulb. Lust's tentative truce? No, this is Passchendaele and the battle is soon in full swing again. Soul's gristle and gore. Affection's infected wound. His arms reach out to me not to embrace me but (oh so gently) to guide me out of the door, safely on to the street, safely out of sight, so that his next client can mount the stairs. Back in my car, its engine sputtering fumes from a rusty exhaust, I make the steady, sad drive home in the sullen evening.

35 A NOTE

To my great surprise a short, handwritten note arrived from my
bishop today by post: 'I'm there with you in spirit and support,
but Christ is there with you in reality and embrace.' I was really
touched by this. Twenty seconds for him; a lifeline for me.

36 LEAVING

I should have left the priesthood years ago. But what would I
do? I haven't enough money to retire, to potter around in the
garden of a home I don't own and couldn't afford to rent or buy.
And my friends? So many of them are priests or involved in the
Church. To sever the chain would be to leave them behind and
leave me out in the cold. It's as if I'm married to the Church and
a divorce would cause my social circle to disintegrate. But if I did
have the courage to walk away what could I do? Teach? I have
my old English degree just like thousands of others (younger,
and with better degrees), but my experience has been exclu-
sively teaching religious studies in a Catholic setting. An older
ex-priest, disgraced and faithless who has worked for no money
and who now needs a salary is hardly going to be inundated with
job offers. Psychotherapy? I know of priests who have hung up
their stoles and trained to be counsellors – the potted plants,
the carpet tiles, the cutesy posters blu-tacked to the walls, yoga
classes in the next room. I couldn't face that smiling world of

self-worth. I need to see a counsellor, not become one. If I could borrow some money I suppose I could open a club somewhere like Pattaya with barely-legal go-go boys dancing on a make-shift stage, for sale by the hour to middle-aged lechers like me. Counting cash as the sun rises, hauling empty beer bottles to the bins, sweeping the rancid floor, cockroaches swilled into the disinfected morning. No, better to die.

I stay a priest because although I am paid a pittance I have a house, a housekeeper, a car, respect, a reason to get up in the morning – although I long ago shifted the 7:30 AM Mass to 10 AM. We still get the same number of (dwindling) communicants. For me now, in the middle-aged wasteland leading up to the scrapheap, there's nowhere else to go. I'm stuck, imprisoned, behind bars. A cleric in fancy dress. A dummy in a stained-glass window. A plaster manikin all dolled up in silk and lace. One push and I'd come crashing down, shattered into smithereens. To walk away presumes feet but I have stumps; it makes it easier to crawl into the cesspit. And anyway it looks as if I will have no choice and will soon have to be 'let go'. This retreat is basically an exam for which the results have already been calculated, a lottery ticket from last month's draw.

But that's not the whole story. I actually feel a priest to my core. I can't really explain it except as an instinct, of care, of protection: an arm around the parish; a mother with her cubs; a conduit for blessings not my own; a bringer of joy not my own; a Jupiter for Planet Earth. Sometimes I'm more like a battered punchbag against which people can vent their rage at life, at God, at the Church. That's fine. I don't mind.

Do I believe in Orders as a sacrament? I don't believe a bishop has the magic power to give me magic powers by the laying on of his hands. Ditto Baptism. God's 'Let there be Light' was said once. Our sacraments retell, not rewrite, that foundational, continuing story. Creation as the Tree of Life has no need to be replanted, only to be pruned and cared for and enjoyed. But I've come to believe in 'priesthood' as a way of transmitting grace. Perhaps it all came from the villages in olden times when the folk took a man from their midst who was spiritually-minded and wise and bestowed on him the authority to be their mediator – a bridge, a connector, with each other as well as with the gods. The priestly office is always above and beyond its holder. And if I refuse to take the medicine it doesn't mean that it won't cure others. The wounded healer again.

Although I've thought of leaving the priesthood and even of leaving the Catholic Church itself, with its rigidity, its fussiness, its excuses, its plain wrong-headed way of looking at so many things, I've never wanted to walk away from Christ. I have recurring questions about who he really was and who he thought he was and who his disciples thought he was, but for me he is still irreplaceable. Suffering, disgrace, death – the three major fears which overshadow human life begin to evaporate in the company of the man from Nazareth. There is no barrel I can scrape where his scratch marks are not there before me.

But beyond the high drama of the Passion is the manger. On a chilly night in a dark place, whilst a busy world was feasting and strutting in decadence and arrogance, a baby bawls and drools and shits in the arms of his unmarried mother. I can't walk away from this. 'It's only a legend,' they say. Maybe. But their confident, dismissive words are inaudible the next street over, never mind beyond the cloak of the one hundred billion stars which glitter across the night sky. Every human life is a legend, but only one outside my own is so personal and so all-encompassing that it seems to share the very blood in my veins, the very air in my lungs.

37   SHAME

Was I ever recognized? Well, Greater Manchester is a large area but safer still was to go out into Merseyside, up into Lancashire, even over the Pennines in the warm summer months when the ride back into a radiant sunset made my melancholy strangely sweet. My safeguard was that the young men I met were unlikely to attend my Masses, especially miles from their home towns. These were the lank-limbed sinners who never darkened the doors of a church, the lost ones who passed by with barely a glance or thought as they lit another cigarette or shuffled to a new song on their smartphones. But there was one time.

I had made contact with a lad in Salford through a website and we'd made a plan to meet. When I arrived ('there's plenty of parking outside') it was a surprisingly fancy building and I

suspected that he was being kept by an older man. I punched
in the code he'd given me and the video camera lit up, followed
immediately by a buzzer. I pushed against the glass door and
entered the sparkling lobby with its marble floors reflecting
intricate chandeliers which drooped down from the high
ceiling. There was a shoe-shining machine next to the lift,
one of those electrical contraptions with three rotating balls
(black, brown and buffer) and a cream dispenser. I pressed the
button to summon the lift and then pressed each of my scruffy
shoes against the nozzle. A white smear oozed on to them and I
activated the whirring brushes. My right foot was quickly clean
and shiny but then the lift door suddenly opened and I could
see that it was controlled directly from the apartment because
the bright sixth-floor button was already illuminated. I hastily
stepped inside as the doors brushed together, my left shoe still
scuffed and still smeared. The lift glided upwards in a smooth
swoop, pinging cheerfully as it passed each floor. I spent the
ascent in a sweat, rubbing the cream off my left shoe with the
back of my trousers.

I preferred the grungy bedsits with their stained carpets and
flimsy walls. This place intimidated me, as if I were about to be
interviewed for a job for which I was unqualified. I stepped out
of the lift into a corridor sweet with the smell of new paint. It
felt just like a hotel and I would not have been surprised to see
a room-service tray outside one of the doors, a silver lid hiding
a half-eaten dinner with a plume of white linen smeared with

ketchup resting there like a dead bird. Why would someone want money for sex with a stranger if they lived in a place like this?

I walked along the hallway, found the apartment and rang its ding-dong bell. The door opened and instantly I recognized Jimmy Cruz, and he me. In a second there took place, like two live electric wires, an exchange of potent energy – amusement on his part, horror on mine. I couldn't have sex with Jimmy Cruz. He'd been in my parish choir as a boy and sung the Christmas solos ('In the Bleak Midwinter'). I'd heard his first Confession. His mother used to help out with my accounts. He fixed my printer once. More recently I'd written him a reference letter when he was applying to university. My body pricked with mortification and shame.

'I . . . I think I'd better go. This is . . . oh God. This is so embarrassing. I'm so sorry Jimmy. I . . .' I mumbled and stammered in a terrible confusion. There was nowhere to hide, physically or morally, and I simply shrivelled into a shell of humiliation.

'It's OK, Father, don't worry,' he said kindly, smiling. 'Why don't you come in and have a cup of tea at least.'

'Oh thanks Jimmy, but I'll just take off.' I was red and hot and I started walking back towards the lift. 'I hope everything's alright. It's . . . been a while,' I said, turning slightly back towards him, my voice sounding strangulated and squeaky, my steps feeling lopsided and awkward. I was going to ask him about university but I didn't really want to know and I certainly didn't want to make our connections any clearer. Would he say anything to anyone? I thought he was decent enough not to make this public but how could he resist at least mentioning it over a drink with his mates?

How desperate I felt as I pressed the button for the lift and sensed that he was still standing in the doorway watching me. Should I say something else? The light above the lift was harsh and unforgiving, like a torch shining into my mouth in a dentist's chair. I looked down at my unevenly polished shoes and listened for the distant mechanical whir, willing it closer. I stood there cringing with awkwardness as if puberty's pimples had all erupted at once on a gawky cheek. I felt as if I were the adolescent and he the mature, confident, successful adult. Finally the lift arrived and the doors opened. 'Bye' I called out as I stepped inside, but there was no response. He must have closed his door and so didn't hear me. It was a quiet, smooth ride down to the ground floor.

38   LIBRARY

The library is the one beautiful room at Craigbourne. Even without reading anything I enjoy its quiet atmosphere, the smell of must and old paper, the gentle chafing sound as I extract a volume from its neighbours.

It has a predictable collection of theology, philosophy and history with some sensible fiction thrown in as a concession to leisure. Fine, hand-tooled books sit next to cheaper hardbacks, originally published with dust jackets but now unclothed – lines of faded spines in washed-out blues, greens or blacks. The classics are here of course, the multi-volumed *Summa* of Aquinas and Butler's *Lives of the Saints*, but there's a wide choice of thoroughbred theological and devotional volumes too, Garrigou-Lagrange, Alphonsus Rodriguez (not the saint), Grou, Dom Chautard, Dom Marmion, Venerable Louis of Granada, St John of the Cross, St Francis de Sales. The mid-20th century lighter-weights, Vann, Chesterton, Sheed and Sheen, sit alongside the heavier, later 20th-century German-language theologians, Rahner, Balthasar and Ratzinger. Surprisingly there are some early Küng and Curran volumes too, flowerings of Vatican II quickly plucked out of the ground by curial authorities in the 1970s and now seeming almost old-fashioned in their earnest modernism. Strange to think of the present silence of books whose contents had fueled decades of vociferous debate. On a separate shelf there is a selection of novels, Mauriac, Bernanos, Undset, R. H. Benson and, curiously, half a dozen beaten-up Tridentine Missals amongst the fiction, their frayed rainbow ribbons betraying a long-past liturgical sell-by date.

I noticed a fat biography of St Alphonsus de Liguori sitting on one of the higher shelves and I climbed the ladder to extract it, taking it to the central, maroon, leather-top table to browse through. My mother kept a prayer-card dedicated to this saint tucked in her missal, a souvenir from a Mission by the Redemptorists in Cork in 1949. I remember it well because the

card often used to slip out during Mass and flutter under the
dusty pew from whence I had to retrieve it. Many of its creases
and scuff marks were formed by my youthful fingers as it was
scratched off the stone floor. On the back was a prayer and on
the front a picture of a kindly-looking, ascetic-looking, gaunt old
man – the 18th-century founder of the Redemptorist Order. His
strange, foreign name stuck in my young mind from this card
and from the frequent singing of one of his hymns at Sunday
afternoon Benediction ('Had I but Mary's sinless heart'), incense
billowing, candles flickering, organ tremulating, Host aloft.
I knew when we'd finished singing St Alphonsus we could go
home in the dark for buttered crumpets and tea by the fire.

I later learned that during the controversies of the centuries
following the Reformation he had helped to make some aspects
of theology flexible again – a spiritual osteopath of sorts.
Jansenism's harsh teachings had laid a heavy weight on frozen
shoulders, God as an iced-over lake rather than living, life-giving
waters. By passionately refuting the idea of predestination, as
well as his writings on moral theology, Alphonsus had helped
make limber and loose again the Body of Christ. As I scanned
the book I was completely amazed at the scope of his life and his
boundless energy as a founder and a bishop. Then I came across
a chapter called 'The Tireless Worker', which described his daily
schedule: ten hours work, eight hours prayer, five hours sleep,
and one hour for eating and recreation. Three days a week only
water, no food, and never eating or drinking between meals, not

even a sip of water during a Neapolitan heatwave. All the food he ate was laced with bitter herbs to make it taste foul, and the fruit he rarely ate was doused with salt. 'I digest it better,' he claimed. He scourged himself daily and it appears he never took off his spiked hair-shirt, even to sleep. Oh, and in his spare time he wrote over a hundred large books – some of them were on the shelves behind me.

I put aside the biography reeling. I felt like a child with a jar of tadpoles standing next to Alexander Fleming with his Petri dish. And my tadpoles were not even alive. But what to say? Was Alphonsus meant to be a model for us? Despite the miracles he reluctantly performed we have no sense of Christ as superhuman. In his very ordinariness lay his authenticity. He fell asleep during the day, he was hungry and satisfied that hunger, he liked hanging out with his close friends: 'Is this not the carpenter's son?' asked the villagers, amazed that he could be anything more elevated than the local odd-job man. But I fear this is just my pathetic excuse. I've set the bar as low as I possibly can in my spiritual life and still I kick it over. Perhaps Alphonsus's way is the only way to be a priest – to jump in at the deep end at the moment of ordination and then never to leave the river. To swim all day long, to sleep on a piece of driftwood, to eat the occasional fish, to survive on air and water. Then it all makes sense. Why would you marry when the stream carries you far from home? Why own anything which you cannot carry on your back and which would perish along the way?

Yet did Alphonsus's life have anything to do with faith as such? It seemed possible to me that he simply chose religion as his preferred form of asceticism rather than athletics or exploration or any number of ways to pour oneself one hundred per cent into life's bottle. And was his distillation of energy into celibacy (not a second in the day free for impure thoughts, his whipped flesh literally bleeding under his cassock) actually the fruit of a disordered sexuality? But who am I to question? The only time blood has flowed down my back was one occasion when I let a tattooed rent boy hit me with a leather belt. The buckle ripped into the flesh of my shoulder. I had to throw away my shirt when I got home, stuffed down low in a plastic bag then stuffed down low in the parish rubbish bin.

Saints rarely offer models for real people. For a start they are almost always sexless, selected and canonized by the sexless, heroes to the sexless. Then they are chosen because their lives are rare examples of a heroism which, by definition, few can match. Which ordinary person can explore the labyrinth of Teresa of Avila's *Interior Castle* without getting lost? And if it's unthinkable to me (obscene even) that Christ would whip himself, why then would his disciples be required or encouraged to take up the scourge? I ascended the ladder again and put Alphonsus back in his place.

Five shelves down was dear Father Faber, early companion and disciple of Cardinal Newman, later enemy and rival of Cardinal Newman: his big heart, Newman's big brain. How I loved Faber's excruciating failure in taste, his exuberance, his violet-scented Victorian piety. He was a roly-poly Italianate wannabe in contrast to Newman, the wizened, whippet-thin Puritan. Newman wrote the great prose; Faber wrote the bad verse: 'Oh happy pyx, oh happy pyx, where Jesus doth his dwelling fix'. But we shouldn't make fun of him (although it's easy to) because his books, despite being ten times longer than necessary, have a wonderful fervour to them – magnanimous, benevolent, encouraging. With Faber there was always room for another chair at the table of the feast, whereas with Newman everyone was expected to stand and eat quickly so he could return alone to his study, a shadow of pained melancholia streaked across his tightened jaw. Nevertheless Faber could be priggish. He once suggested we should pray for rain on bank holidays so people would avoid sin by staying indoors – surely the most bizarre misjudgment of people and of sin and of the circumstances of their interaction. Both Newman and Faber were almost certainly gay but whereas Newman kept Ambrose St John, his lifelong special friend, at a controlling, Oxbridgian distance (despite insisting that they share a grave together), Faber sublimated his homosexuality with an excessive Mariolatry. Whether dressing up the statue of Our Lady in the most outrageous lace or singing her praises to the very edge of blasphemy he loved Mary as a later generation would love Judy Garland. The Blessed Virgin: a gay icon for celibate gay priests; the untouchable Woman for those who had no desire to touch women.

I put all the books back on the shelves but was not yet ready to return to my room so I went over to sit in one of the leather chairs by the window and look out at the garden. The rain splashing on to piles of wet, brown leaves on the ground. The rain dripping down the windowpane to its rotting, blackened base. My winding-down, my draining-off, my giving-up – my compost conscience, all mulch. 'The kingdom of heaven is like a merchant seeking fine pearls, and upon finding one pearl of great value he went and sold all that he had and bought it.' Here in this room the secret treasures of the interior life need not be sought because they are within a mere reach of an arm, to be revealed, possessed. The only cost is the desire to begin and the will to continue. I have neither. I have nothing to sacrifice except sex. But that's what I seek. I am a merchant in search of fine pearls of pleasure. Orgasms seem to me so much more alluring than prayer and I've sold my soul to procure them. 'Say only the word and my soul shall be healed.' The word. One word. But I sit, tongue-tied at the darkening window. My only words are the words I write now as afternoon fails and evening falls.

39 FARHAN

There were rich pickings to be found all over the suburbs of Manchester and Liverpool and Leeds, countless sordid staircases leading up to countless student bedsits. The flats above the fish and chip shops or kebab joints with the smell of frying batter or burning meat blending in a halo of lust with Armani's Aqua di Gio or Jean Paul Gaultier's Le Male.

I've had boys who were so good-looking I couldn't perform, perfect features, bodies like athletes, smiles like the sun at noon. Then there were others who were completely repulsive to me, those whose unwashed armpits or groins left me gagging, those who spat foul-breathed lies of passion out of sticky, white-crusted lips, those with acne that was weeping, backs sprouting with spots all smeared with blood and discharge. The overly effeminate were always a turn-off, wispy creatures with wimpy bodies: 'Oh you naughty, naughty boy', they would pout. 'You're getting me all hot and bothered. What's a gurl to do!' The fat ones, all blubber; the thin ones like leafless twigs. The photographs or descriptions on the internet were often deceptive: hot, hung and horny could turn out to be a listless, disinterested lout with a penis the size of a clothes peg.

The most upsetting though was Farhan from Bangladesh. I climbed up the stairway to his flat in Oldham, its swirling red carpet pitted with stains and threadbare on the edge of every step. The thin front door with an open slit for post (no cover) let out a smell of curry and the sound (God help me!) of a baby crying. Dark-skinned, wiry, intensely handsome, he opened the door and graciously invited me into the flat. It was a total mess, clothes strewn everywhere. On the right a small kitchen area was piled high with dishes and on the far left sat a pretty, young woman, presumably his wife. At her feet two young children were playing with some toys and behind them was a crib with a baby wriggling inside. The wife seemed frightened and embarrassed but the kids looked up at me grinning, their eyes all open in wonder and innocence. My heart shredded inside me with shame and pity. I almost thought of changing the plan, of going over to the children and joining in their game, of chatting to the mother, finding out how long she'd been in the country, how things were going, how the kids were enjoying school, what their names were. In short, to be a priest, a pastor, a joy-bringer. The embers of my old vocation stirred into flame but Farhan was already standing at the bedroom door. It was somehow too late to change direction. The plane had accelerated along the runway to the point of take-off and could not be halted. I smiled at the mother and children and mumbled a prayer for this little family group, so tender, so full of hope, then picked my way through the debris to the bedroom.

Farhan closed the door and looked at me, coyly, teasingly, as if with real sexual desire. Could it be? Maybe he was bisexual? Maybe he enjoyed having sex with men? Maybe he was in an arranged marriage and things were different in his culture? I trampled down my doubts and began to form some strange fantasy that I was helping Farhan and his family by having sex with him in their bedroom. Well, I suppose I would be giving them more money in the next hour than he would otherwise earn in a day. He reached over and started to undress me, button by button, kissing me, touching me.

I could see the lump of an erection in his jeans. At least I knew I was not the first man to be with him in this room. This was someone who was experienced and comfortable with sex.

It was a wildly passionate session and I was embarrassed by the noises he made, which had to have been audible in the next room despite the jingle of cartoons on the television. 'You don't need to' I wanted to tell him, but he continued and I turned a horrible corner where the fact that we were being overheard actually made the whole experience more exciting. You can snuff out a moral light, pinch dead the stamen of conscience when one body is squeezing pleasure out of another, deep down into the bone.

We finished, his lean, taut body glistening with sweat and as beautiful as a statue, and he went over to the corner to get some paper towels. My sense of unease suddenly returned and I dreaded the walk through the living room, past the kids with the toys, the baby in the crib, the mother with the frightened eyes. I saw one of her bras on the floor under his dark brown feet as he leant over to wipe off my body and I was overcome with sadness. I dressed and paid him and opened the bedroom door. The wife was now standing at the stove on the left, stirring a large steel pot on the flame. She didn't turn around. 'Bye-bye' cried one of the little urchins, waving at me. He looked just like his father. 'Bye-bye' I replied awkwardly, walking swiftly across the room to the front door. It squeaked as I opened it and slammed shut coldly. The swirls in the red carpet made me dizzy as I went downstairs in despair and misery. There was a distant squeal of delight from one of the kids upstairs. Dinner time. The theme music for Bugs Bunny with its rapid xylophone riff began playing on the television. I walked to my car in the darkness.

40 HALFWAY

Halfway through the retreat. I'm used now to the blank spaces of each day, the lack of conversation, the absence of my mobile phone and the internet. My first days here were dark. Cold turkey. But now . . . I can't say I feel at peace but I'm somewhere between numb and resigned. Peace is outside the window. I know it's there even if I don't experience it. That gives me some sort of contentment. I feel less lonely too even though I hardly notice the other retreatants. We sit at the same large table at mealtimes and we concelebrate Mass every morning but otherwise they're just shadows in the corridors, a scuffle of a chair behind a bedroom wall.

Soon I'll be back home and will have to face that storm which is likely to destroy me. The hurricane is creeping up the coast. But what is the alternative? To stay safely hidden away somewhere like Craigbourne for the rest of my life? Just writing that makes me flinch with dread. Yet I'm so stupid! I'm facing total ruination, complete disgrace beyond imagining, my naked body all over the internet, front page spreads in the Sunday tabloids – ridicule, poverty. I've lost everything but despite having a disease I can't accept the cure. I cling to my sickness as if I would die without it. It's *my* cancer. If you take that away what's left of me? I can't see that if I could only let go then everything might be reborn.

Fear of Hell might be able to stop some people from habitual sin but when you're already sinking in the mud repentance seems as impossible as jumping out of a window and flying through the air. My situation now isn't that I've taken the wrong path, it's that I'm stationary with no legs. The eager pushing along by Father Neville is a pushing over. Step by step to holiness . . . for those with feet. That's why a bullying religion is so useless. You can't force open fingers without snapping bones, you must caress until the digits loosen.

'Stretch out your hand!' Christ once said to a paralyzed man. I hear him say it to me now. Can I hope that one day will and muscle will be united and that my withered limb can be made whole? This thought at least keeps the bandage in place; it allows some ray of light into the sepulchre.

41   THE WOMAN

The woman caught in the act (the mind boggles) of adultery. Men (of course), callous, brutal, prurient, burst into the room. She is naked. Breasts glistening and glowing, blood rushing through her veins. He is inside her. Suddenly, men are at the bedside. 'You slut!' Slap-dragged out of the sheets. Bodies wet. Clothes pulled on. Hair wild. Armpits rank. The man (quicker for him to dress) stumbles then runs away. Or maybe she was not fully naked? Maybe it was a quick slake of carnal desire – sex snatched after lunch? Or perhaps she was being raped? Dress hitched up as she struggled. Pants ripped down just low enough for entry. The crude grope. Pinned back. Slit found. Pushed in. Deep past the raw. Fuck. Gasp. Spurt. Out. Gone. Man's two-minute pleasure for woman's nine-month pain.

She is manhandled to the town square and flung down before Jesus, her dress torn and bloody. Her eyes are wild with fear and shame but there is still some sass in the dark-shadowed face. The dregs of hauteur are not yet fully dry. One layer of skin is still left to cover the ignominy. One thread prevents her final slip into the abyss. Their fingers point. Accusing. Condemning. Mocking. Outraged. Scandalized. How *dare* she?

Jesus. Doodling in the dust. Killing time. Wait…is that naughts and crosses? He looks up distractedly, disturbed in his reverie. 'What's up, guys? Oh, I see. Yeah, I guess you're right. OK. The one who's not sinned amongst you. Let him throw the first stone.' He goes back to his doodling, looking at the ground as if in a daze. Is he stoned? Is he simple? The men are coiled with anger. Amos picks up a choice stone, with sharp edges. As his arm draws back to muster full force he glances over again at Jesus who suddenly looks up, now alert as a spark, eyes like flint boring into Amos' soul. He squeezes the stone in his claw-like fist, then…drops it with a plop to the ground, eyes shifty. 'Heretic!' he mumbles angrily under his breath as he walks away, kicking other stones in his path. The others follow suit, one by one, a humiliated procession, fury's coitus interruptus, blue balls.

Jesus is still sitting on the ground, alone now with the woman. She is sweating, dishevelled, trembling. 'Where have they all gone?' he asks, half-smiling and looking around in mock surprise. 'Has no one cast a stone? Has no one condemned you, after all of that?' Her heart opens up cautiously like a flower. 'No one, sir.' She waits for him to pick up a stone himself but he is still doodling in the dust, tracing lines in that powder which survives when all stones have been worn away. 'Well I don't condemn you either. Go now in peace but for heaven's sake don't get yourself into that mess again!' He smiles at her and then looks down at the ground again, his palm now smoothing away the ridges in the sand.

She hesitates. She wants to hug him but she's afraid, dirty, shy, so she turns and quickly runs away to wash her body now that her soul is clean. She has tears flooding down her cheeks.

I put down my pen. I have tears flooding down my cheeks.

42 CONFESSION

Many who are not priests misunderstand the sacrament of Confession. They think it's a time of lurid fascination, an episode of a private soap opera, shameful beans spilled in a shadowy space. Actually most priests find hearing Confessions to be one of the duller, more tedious parts of their ministry. Sins are monotonous and mundane. In more recent years we have been trained in counselling and speak of Reconciliation rather than Confession, of 'changing the direction in which you search for happiness' rather than 'doing penance for sin'. Good intentions, a nice try, but most people just want to get in and out of the box as fast as possible, a quick-wash setting. They talk in euphemisms: 'gossip', 'lustful thoughts and actions', 'angry words', 'lies'. Many don't really want to change habits of sin, they just want a temporary clean slate – a washable nappy, white until the next soiling and the next laundering. Many times I've spun what I thought was an inspired spiel of encouragement only to sense a mounting impatience on the other side of the partition.

When people come with heavy burdens it's enriching to be able to bring relief. Merely for them to speak their tortured thoughts, to share a secret in confidence, can be a comfort. But some (older women in particular) are comfortless because their souls are scarred with scruples. Nothing they do brings them peace, and nothing I say can break through the crust of guilt. Every passing thought has the potential to become a new sin requiring another Confession to remove it. Like a bucket with a constant drip from a leaking tap, the bottom is never dry. One sad old lady used to come to me almost every day for Absolution and any attempt by me to show her the false nature of this under-standing of God and sin was itself a temptation in her eyes. If you believe the Devil is out to get you at every step then every step is a dance with Satan.

I've never felt the remotest desire to betray the seal of Confession. Even here I would not write down anything private. We were told in the novitiate the (possibly fictional) story of a priest visiting a university who was telling the students about his first time hearing Confessions. 'I had a baptism of fire. I was only in the box for *two minutes* and a man came in to confess that he had raped an under-age girl and then had persuaded her to have an abortion. That's quite a debut for a newly-ordained priest.' Then, at the end of the lecture, before the students had left, one of the senior professors came into the room to meet the priest. 'Hello Father. Good to see you again after so many years. You won't remember this but I was your first penitent immediately after you were ordained.'

I've seen people leave the box with tears of joy. Others have left enraged, like the man who had stolen a large sum of money from his employer. I insisted he would have to pay it back as soon as he was able. He stormed out, carrying his sins with him. Such is the sacrament. Without a firm purpose of amendment the words of Absolution are meaningless. Sacraments are not magic; they do not conjure rabbits out of hats. They do not make new planets from scratch. They help heal the brokenness of our own already-existing world and remind us to cherish the beauty of our planet ... and of our rabbits. The Communion wafer couldn't be changed into a gold coin, the Communion wine couldn't become a quiver of mercury, but they both become *our* flesh and blood as we digest them. And the ritual itself awakens the memory of a foundational meal of total self-giving: 'Do this in memory of me.' The 'this' is complete self-donation, not a conjuring trick.

The priest doesn't change the state of anyone's soul as much as he facilitates a change of heart. 'Go, your sins are forgiven' is, I think, a declaration of something which has already happened, not its cause. And 'Go' is the important word: get on your journey, and let go. It is a similar case with Baptism. When I pour water over the baby's head it's more for my benefit and the parents' benefit and the community's benefit than for the infant's. It reminds those of us who are witnessing the ceremony that God already loves this child as he loves every child he created. If God has chosen this baby to be his own then how can we reject it? Baptism celebrates the embrace by God (already given nine months earlier) of yet another newly-born beloved son or daughter in whom he is well pleased.

43   THE LINE

I remember a summer weekend in London when I was helping out a priest friend. During a long aimless walk on a hot Saturday evening I came across The Line, a sleazy-looking gay club which spilled thudding music out of a half-open door. I was curious so I stepped inside and passed down a staircase from the balmy semi-darkness of the street to the air-conditioned murk below. Everything was streaked with flashing lights, illuminations revealing in jerks of manic brilliance the walls of thin, flaking black paint. I felt the traction of sticky spilt drinks on the floor as I made an awkward path towards the bar. Boy dancers wearing tight shorts strutted or stood around, their dazed eyes scouring the room for clients, hoping for that ten pound note to be tucked into their elasticized waistbands, the scratch of stiff paper against the shaved pubic hair followed by an entitled brush against the bulge. I was happy just to watch, cradling a bottle of beer in the shadows.

Why was it so dark? 'Men loved darkness rather than light, because their deeds were evil,' says the Gospel. I'm not sure that that really applied here. Darkness in The Line was facilitation, or a mask – the pretence of beauty unseen in the shadows. In harsh supermarket light the dry skin would show its blotches, the acne its deeper crevices and scars, the scared eyes their fear and weariness. Here the gloom gave everyone easy fantasies.

Of course I arrived too early. These places come to life in the small, dead hours, a pulsating space under cities when most people are asleep. I only stayed until 11:30 as I had a Mass to celebrate the next morning. Strange to think of my congregation tucked up in warm duvets and chaste embraces as I stood alongside the bar, my one beer becoming ever flatter and warmer, its metallic label picked at and peeling off. When I would be standing at the altar at eight o'clock the next morning those yet to arrive at The Line would be staggering home, T-shirts sweat-damp which had begun the evening stretched clean and white over gym-toned bodies. Men flopping dizzily on to strange beds with teeth unbrushed – room spinning, underwear a spewed,

moist tangle on the floor, all dark behind the shameless morning
curtains. The cycle, the treadmill: washing-wearing-dirtying-
washing; arousal-orgasm-disgust-arousal – sperm's lemming-like
swim before reincarnation.

I left and took the music with me. What had been throbbing
out of speakers now filled my head as I climbed the stairs back
up to London's streets. Rhythm's fake heartbeat: all is well, all is
healthy, blood in the veins, colour in the cheeks. I took the Tube
back to Kilburn and knew I would be tired and depressed at Mass
eight hours later, but when morning arrived (6:50 alarm, a cup of
strong tea, early sun on the small lawn, chirping, merry birds) its
freshness, which I had expected to be an accusation of innocence
scorned, was like a kind smile from a saner world. I would read
the liturgical texts word for word without feeling or faith but
something calm, a fragile peace, fell over me. My spiritual life
was a bush hacked to the ground with blunt shears, but under the
mashed branches, in the undergrowth, sap was flowing.

44   THE JEWS GOT IT RIGHT

You can't undo a Jew. Regardless of the level of observance or
belief you cannot be removed from the planet which is your
Jewishness. There's wisdom in this. Yes, the Law requires
hundreds of behavioural observances of deed and diet and dress,
but all within the context of being already accepted, chosen,
loved . . . safe. Christianity soon replaced this with mental assent

to creeds and dogmas. I wrote something about this earlier this week – what does it mean to believe or to be 'saved'? Grace was meant to complete the Law (creating a universal Judaism – all were chosen) but this grace came to require either Catholic absence of sin (and the cult of saints who alone, whether at death or after Purgatory, could enter Heaven), or the Protestant's 'faith alone', on which Luther built his mighty fortress and which required one Big Assent, after which all was well. Both of these Christian paths have loose stones to trip us up. Am I holy (sinless) enough? Did I believe (assent) enough? Never enough. God with the measuring rod. God with the account book. God separating the sheep from the goats. But sheep cannot not be sheep; and you can't undo a Jew.

Christianity was never meant to suggest that 'Now we have a better religion than Judaism', but rather 'Now everyone can be a Jew – all are invited to the party.' That's Gospel, Good News ... nothing gooder. But soon Christians tried to stop the party. They went about throwing out the original guests (hosts). They made everyone play intricate party games, the esoteric rules of which no one quite understood, games invented in foreign places such as Athens or Rome. A Jew only needs to wake up and become conscious of being Jewish to be saved: 'What is this air I breathe? Ah yes, the breath of God!' To exist is to be cherished. Simple. The Law is merely an aid to focus, a way to be attentive to the foundational blessing, a reminder that we are loved into life, an encouragement to savour rather than gobble at the feast. The Church's 'new commandment' of love became (too often) a *path* to being accepted rather than the joyful fruit of it. My mother's rosary beads rattling like moneychangers' coins in the Temple. Haven't you heard the Good News? 'Yea, come, buy wine and milk without money and without price.' Isaiah already knew it. Currency's finished. Everything belongs to everyone. It is the air we breathe. Goats are extinct.

45   FEELINGS

Following on from my musing this morning on the Jews and accepting our acceptance by the One who created us, my mind goes back to my novitiate year and the suspicion we were told to have of 'feelings', especially when related to the spiritual life. 'You should not look for consolation in prayer. A sign that you are making progress is to experience darkness when meditating. All the saints went through this. It's so that you will seek the God of consolations not the consolations of God.' This was a recipe for neurosis for me because when I did feel a glow in the chapel, a sense of the love of God, my instant reaction was to step away from its midday sun and try to seek instead to enter into the Dark Night of the Soul with St John of the Cross as guide. To enjoy feeling close to God seemed like a failure in generosity towards God. Prayer which was distasteful was, I imagined, automatically more effective.

Of course this is screwed up but too often so is the traditional striving for holiness. Countless bitter, depressed celibates have cultivated this strange psychosis of the spirit to console themselves in a desolation caused not by an affirming of the divine but by a denial of the human. After they have stripped the flesh (sometimes quite literally) of its feelings they then view the resulting desiccation as God's will and as a sign of his favour. To be a spiritual skeleton, heart removed, hardened with self-control, is the way to sanctity; physical mortification is the prayer of the body, a sharing in the Passion of Christ.

This places us on a knife-edge of scruples because if we take pride or pleasure in mortifications we immediately undo any benefit they might bring us. But to choose suffering (suffering which chooses us is a different question) has to mean on some level that we do take pleasure in it – sadomasochism is always lurking inside monastery walls. The only sane response to pain is to reject it; such an instinct is written deep in our souls, in our bodies. A cut begins to heal as soon as the dagger is withdrawn. Deliberately to create pain for ourselves for its own sake (for God's sake!) is to insult the Universe. And heirs to the throne do not need to crawl on their bloodied knees at the city gates.

Yet how do we take care of the flesh, embrace the flesh, without being smothered by the flesh?

46   GOONG

That boy from Laos. Goong. He had travelled far to study computer science at Manchester University. Poor, face of smiles, spotless, elegant, every gesture seeming as natural in its undulation as a river's deft sway from verdant bank to forest's secret hiding place. He bowed low in greeting and undressed me gently, every shirt button teased slowly from its hole with his long, slender fingers. He tugged on and then released my jeans' stuck zipper, kneeling down with a chuckle to get a better angle on the metal teeth's halting descent. He then stood up and took me into his thin arms with reverence, as if holding a sacred vessel. With the Western men I'd met there was always something rough or resentful or distracted or routine about the encounter. With Goong I felt connected to a culture where sexual expression was a natural part of being a human being, a sharing of pleasurable space. I felt within a minute (no more) that we could simply be together with no guilt, no past, no future, no ownership, just together in a room with enough oxygen for both of us. We didn't need more. I didn't even need sex.

Was it Buddhism? The harmony of existence. Not pushing inexorably towards eternity's long stretch ahead (Heaven or Hell) but rather reincarnation's phlegmatic, circular pull. A sphere with no markers, a universe of calm, unruffled energy. G. K. Chesterton wrote of the difference between Christianity and Buddhism as between the Cross and the Circle, one pointing with purpose upwards and outwards, the other a prison turned in on itself, a soulless, static globe. The Cross certainly inspired spectacular achievements (universities, hospitals, orphanages, masterpieces of art, inventions of science) but at that moment in Goong's digs, as our planet groans and shudders from Christendom's raping excavations and explorations, I felt supremely happy in the perfect circle of our intimacy. Not just happy, but blessed and cherished as we celebrated each other's bodies without possessiveness. I would leave, he would leave, but for one hour of the giant Circle's rotation we had had a feast. And we had smiled. I've seen grins and leers on rent boys' faces but Goong's smile was sacramental. It was, as with Moses face to face with the burning bush, a glow reflecting the Divine.

We finished (he wouldn't let me get off the bed until he had cleansed me with a warm, damp towel) and I paid him. He took the money with another gentle bow and smile. It would feed him and it would feed his family back in Laos. For once I couldn't see the sin. His bedroom seemed filled with angels.

47   MASS

As a priest my first job is to celebrate the Mass. We were told in seminary that everything else can be done by anyone else, but only a priest can change bread and wine into the body and blood of Christ. When I was first ordained – fingers trembling as they held the wafer, petrified in case my intention to consecrate was weak or compromised or that I was in a state of sin which might invalidate the process – it was me and the wheat. The Host a pure circle between my thumb and forefinger, my hands a cradle for the miracle. Others were in attendance but my job was simply to do what I was doing, to allow grace to be transmitted to them from the sacred space. New theological ideas (in the Church and in me) changed the focus. The priest now stood alongside the congregation in a bigger circle, the circle of existence itself, in a cradle of limitless grace beyond sight and sense. The altar was like a circular table gently, graciously turned. We were at a banquet which was perpetually replenished, with no one left hungry.

I re-read the words of institution I've said at least ten thousand times. 'He broke the bread, gave it to his disciples, and said: Take this, all of you, and eat it; this is my body which will be given up for you.' But something else is going on here. Imagine the scene. THIS (breaking the bread) MY BODY. It's a mime – flesh torn apart. THIS (pouring some wine) MY BLOOD. It's a mime – red liquid flowing. Not so much the change of one element to another but Jesus playing charades, representing the manner of his death in a theatrical tableau. DO THIS IN MEMORY OF ME – enact the mime once more, let the snap of bread and drip of wine remind you of my death, my self-giving. At Emmaus the 'crack' of the bread at supper was enough to open the eyes of the disciples. They knew it was him with no need for words.

TAKE, EAT – chew, then defecate. TAKE, DRINK – swallow, then urinate. Bread and wine become God, then God becomes shit and piss. Another circle of existence – the ultimate humiliation. But *humus* is Latin for earth, from which we come and to which we go. Don't be afraid of dirt and decay and death. Life is a charade but it's all we have and it's all we need.

I suppose it's an addiction – to sex, to danger, even to sleaze. I know what the homeless must feel sleeping with a mangy dog and a half-empty bottle of cheap booze next to their filthy blankets. The energy to reform is not there because we've become convinced that the addiction itself provides energy in its purest form. My addiction is not visible or obviously anti-social. I just need my regular fix, usually on Tuesdays, my day off. But if for some reason it doesn't work out I become furious inside, like a child deprived of a favourite toy. On those occasions I could sweep my desk clear with rage. I could gnaw my knuckles to the bone in sheer frustration. I don't answer the phone for at least a couple of hours before I need to get into my car. The answering machine takes the messages – the head-teacher wondering when he can talk to me about the next parents' meeting, or the desperate voice of a mother wanting me to visit her sick child. Not on a Tuesday afternoon. Sorry, no way!

I've never actually had sex in my car but that metal box is the prelude and postlude to most of my carnal encounters. The drive to the boy, grasping the wheel, clutch catching the riding gears, smooth swoop round corners, traffic lights winking along my path to pleasure. And then afterwards, the contrast. Slumped in the grimy seat, the grind of return, the stopping and starting, the greasy windows, the dust-encrusted dashboard, the muddy mat under my feet, the belch of fumes with each slow acceleration. All in the same rectangular box.

The outbound journey is not without anxiety, though. Getting there on time, finding the address – my sat nav's memory is a record of my orgasmic history. I am usually early and I sit in my parked car, the minutes passing, looking at the clock, surveying the path, checking the message again on my phone, imagining the first fumble, the first wet lip, my head soon to be buried in his dank groin, pig at a trough. Four minutes to go, keys out of ignition, hands moist, a shake of the knee, a fifth glance in the overtaking mirror, check my teeth, pop in a breath-mint, smooth down my hair, practise one more smile, swing legs out of the car, door gently closed, locked, keys pocketed. A quick look around (anonymity assured), then a nonchalant walk to the carefully memorized address.

But sometimes things do not go to plan, I'm there, I've parked, I find the front door, I press the bell . . . and there's no answer. Buzzing and buzzing, checking the address a dozen times, phoning again and again, the brick wall of voicemail, back to the car, returning home with a full tank of sperm. Nothing can describe the emptiness I feel, a rush followed by a crash. I can be lonely and desolate after an hour of passion (I often am), but the fall to the ground is more gentle. The body is relaxed and de-stressed and the perfume of the fantasy lingers. I can still chase it with my nose. But the no-show is a sort of redundancy without pay, a stock wiped clean off the market without dividend.

I try not to repeat an encounter, at least not for a number of months – variety is part of the thrill. And the unknown.

A stranger's body, his unique map of moles, the shape of his calves, the bend of his dick, the taste of his sweat. There are many disappointments, men who are unattractive or (yes, worse) not into it. To realize someone is simply going through the motions is a real turn-off. The best prostitutes are the ones who make you believe you're the best punter they've ever had, who make you think that they are actually attracted to you, that somehow your paunch and greasy pate (that mountainous stomach and moist, follicle desert) are wildly sexy to this slender youth.

So let me think, if I've been going for my fuck-fix once a week for about five years then that's almost three hundred...no, surely not. How could there be so many? Well, there are repeat visits of course, but still I'm astonished by the arithmetic. So many faces and bodies, few of which I can remember. What's mad is that I actually sympathize with the Church's teaching. I know what I'm doing isn't good. You can't rewrite the moral theology textbooks to include the sanctification of casual sex. Although maybe you can – and who cares about those wretched manuals anyway? I've prayed many times for a man who was peeling off his body-hugging underpants, Superman stretched over the bulging crotch then cast down on the floor. I've reclined on a strange bed, sheets drenched with semen and sweat, mine and his, and felt my heart reach out with compassion and tenderness. I've wanted to stand up and preach the love of God with a used condom rather than a crucifix in my hand.

I'm addicted to the pleasure, of course. The big bang of orgasm. Then the vague hope of a tenderness which will give that orgasm a bigger bang. A hit, they call it, when heroin floods the vein – brain to dick in an arterial shoot. But beyond the neurological fact of my firing dopamine cylinders I've also become addicted (this is sick) to the degradation itself. The Gethsemane of the barbed-wire fence through which I drag myself time after time after scar after scar – emotional wounds hardened yet still scratched to blood. The search for meaning on a scrambled screen, then the dazed, delirious glare at the jumbled letters and their empty message. I've grown to love the wrench of fake caresses, a bulimic abuse which heaves my stomach inside-out in a nausea of lust. I wallow in that post-coital interlude – shot, sucked-dry, the penis's limp repose, the flaccid seconds ticking away until it can be aroused to rigidity once more and teased up to the tipping point of another orgasm.

My loneliness itself ends up being a comfort, a clarity in the mist. Pain's truth too, emotional pain but also the red-raw rash where intercourse scratches me dry. Impaled. Sinking lower as he pushes deeper. A gouging of spirit, my anus an eye socket scraped empty of sight.

49   FAKE

My whole life is a fake, so much dishonesty, so many lies. A living lie in fact. Nothing is authentic. There have been days when every word out of my mouth was false, all sawdust and broken glass. No one really knows me. I act the whole time. I bend down to play with children but I dislike children. I smile at people but I'm full of distaste for them. I explain the miracles in John's Gospel to the secondary school assembly but I don't believe they happened. I go to a parishioner's home after a funeral and select comforting words as someone might select a tie to match a shirt. Everything's a sham. I'm waterproof. A hurricane of distress around me but making sure I remain dry. Is everyone secretly like this? Surely there have to be people who live authentically, whose gestures and words have a ring (lovely word) of truth about them. Repentance? I can't even stay pure during Confession: 'Bless me, Father. I have sinned. In my last Confession I had no contrition or purpose of amendment. And I'm not sure I'm sorry now that I wasn't sorry then.' A terrible, dizzy circle of mendacity. 'Physician, heal thyself.' But how? Administer the last sleeping pills? Cut out the cancer of the heart which is life itself?

If I said all of this to a sympathetic priest he could probably bring some comfort. 'Father Joseph, I'm not going to tell you that these are temptations because you know that. I'm not going to assure you that nothing can come between you and the love of God, or that nothing is beyond hope and healing, or that a mere glance in the direction of Christ is enough, or that it is at this very point of darkness that you are being offered the light of grace. You know all of these things, Father.' Of course I do, I can write the script for that priest. I am doing it now. That's the problem, I know the answers to my own questions.

Nevertheless, despite my anger and frustration here at Craig-bourne, at least I'm trying to remove some of the varnish and strip down to the grain – despite the risk that when one's whole life is a veneer there may be no grain left to uncover. Sanding down and down...worn down, a pile of dust mounting at my side and the edifice that is me slowly reduced to nothing.

But has my life really been so useless, so unremittingly depressing as these notes suggest? Father Neville asked me yesterday to make a list of positive things that have happened since I became a priest, blessings received from God as well as blessings I've shared with others, ways my ministry has made an impact in my parishioners' lives. This is harder for me to do than cataloguing my sins. I'm used to self-examination meaning what's wrong rather than what's right. I remember a priest in Confession once asking me what I'd done over the past month about which I was proud rather than ashamed. My immediate reaction, after a wince of embarrassment, was that I could think of nothing; and then as things popped into my mind I was too shy to mention them. It seemed so crass to talk about my flimsy virtues, to try to list the paltry good deeds I'd done with such mixed motives, like a sort of pathetic self-justification: 'I held the balls of Dimitri as his cock was pressed against my tonsils but...oh yeah, I did hold the hand of that frightened woman in the hospital bed the night before her amputation. Both legs.'

But now I think about it I suppose I can recall moments of self-giving in my life (this is so hard for me to write down).

I do visit my parishioners regularly, especially if they are in hospital. Yes, three times a week for a couple of hours in the evening I am there at Altrincham General, going from bedside to bedside, listening to the woes of the patients, trying to lift spirits. I continue to visit the nursing home where my mother was living until her death and spend some time talking to the residents. I put aside some money every week for an orphanage in India. I clean and tidy up a bit before my housekeeper arrives so she will have less to do. I'm good with older women, those facing hard times after bereavement or marital breakdown. I never turn away anyone who knocks at the presbytery door. I give up my seat on the bus to the elderly. I'm nice to super-market check-out girls. I smile at babies in prams...God! The descent into banality. My greatest virtue must be to feel a surge of nausea in my gut as I write down this saccharine shit.

I'm sorry but there's something obscene about raking around for scraps of gold amongst our daily dross, even if it's still worse to rake around in order to probe the dung – and then to be disappointed when it no longer stinks, like missing a scab that's healed and which can no longer fascinate as we pick at its crust. Self-forgetfulness is the ideal, which treads both virtue and vice underfoot as it walks towards another's needs. The luminous good works of patience and kindness are like music which you can't see or hold or possess – vibrating for a while, then remaining only in the memory. Virtues never belong to us. They are always beyond our grasp.

I came across these words of Christ in St Mark's Gospel just now: 'Whoever believes and is baptized will be saved, but whoever does not believe will be condemned. These signs will accompany those who believe: they will handle serpents; if they drink poison it will not harm them; they shall lay hands on the sick, and they shall recover.'

Serpents, poison, sickness...wait a minute! This simply isn't true. People today, believers or not, are not unharmed if they drink arsenic or grasp cobras. Nor do Christians go around laying hands on the sick and watching them recover. I know people claim such healings take place (and the jury's out for me on Lourdes) but that's not what the Gospel is saying anyway. It doesn't suggest that these things can happen, it claims they will happen, as a matter of course. And, moreover, not only that these things will happen but that these are the very signs which will distinguish those on their way to Heaven from those on their way to Hell. The context makes that clear.

So if the claims about serpents, poison and sickness are untrue then perhaps the claims about being saved and damned are untrue too, or at least not quite so clear. Maybe 'believe' is a broader concept than we think – and perhaps there are other ways to think of the three witchdoctor acts than might at first be apparent.

'Believing' in Christ is to 'put on the mind of Christ', as St Paul puts it, not simply to affirm him or to accept a dogma.

I can see my mother's eyes rolling at this liberal bending around the plain sense of the words but I never saw her swallowing bleach, nor could she bring my father back to life as he lay pulped under the bus on their honeymoon.

To condemn is to be condemned: is this the infamous 'unforgivable sin against the Holy Spirit'? The guilt of one who maintains there is an unforgivable sin in the first place, who fails to condemn the very idea of condemnation. Surely such a person has indeed failed to 'put on the mind of Christ'?

— Handling serpents: subduing violence and hatred, overcoming them with love.
— Drinking poison: absorbing the venom around us, keeping our peace then sharing that peace.
— Laying hands on the sick: touching others with kindness beyond words, a balm for those whom medicines cannot reach.

51   DEATH AND HELL

I've always been afraid of dying; yet on other days, in the blear between sleeping and waking, I actually long for death. Not (if only!) like confident St Paul: 'To live is Christ, to die is gain.' For me to live is emptiness when it's not panic, and to die would be to be finished with both. As I half-wake from my narcotic dreams I want instantly to return to them, a soggy crouton sunk deep-down under a thick pea soup. Sleep as permanent hibernation with no seasons to arouse me, dark as a pillow pressed into heavy eyelids.

On other days, more decisively, more chillingly, I realize I could choose never to have to fear death again. I could choose to extinguish my life like a candle, to make a final exit from the stage, to release the safety curtain's catch one last time as the audience crowds away from the theatre to the laughter and comfort of their homes. Lights low. Temperature cooling like a corpse. I could turn off the refrigerator one last time, empty out the last pot of marmalade, the last wedge of dried-out cheese, the last shrivelled carrot, the last curdling carton of milk, and move the dial to OFF for ever. No more of life's groceries, life's queueing up to pay, life's schlepping shopping home, life's diminishing supplies constantly in need of replenishing. Switch off, then the swish of a gently-closed, vacuum-sealed door.

But there are some good days, energetic days, when there is heartrending regret at the thought of eventually having to part for ever from life's jubilant feast, the dread of dying as a physical flinch, as an ache of longing. The fridge is full, its shelves are bowed: 'Let's have a party!' The sheer celebration of mere existence: every tree's branches outflung with joy; every surge of floral colour; the giggle of surf at the ocean coast; the smile of sun on dipping sea.

However, when death does come, on the other side of its final door there awaits the Christian judgement, Heaven or Hell, the most serious seriousness. No escape. I've reached the last

Dead End. And then it begins. *Anfangen!* All the things God forbade us to do to others he permits to be done to us...without ceasing. The endless pain, the excruciating torture, the extinguished hope, the vanquished compassion, the closed ear. 'Lord, how many times shall I forgive the one who sins against me? Seven times?' 'Not seven times but seventy-seven times,' said Christ. Yet now we find ourselves accused of a seventy-eighth sin. No, it can't be. The dead end has to have an exit.

And it does! Back to the beginning. The foundational story. Abraham and Isaac. Just as it was utterly impossible that God would *really* want Abraham to kill his son (sit with the concept, see beyond the words on the page), so the idea of God creating a universe in which going to Hell is possible is...impossible. Impossible! Ah, but that's it! That's the solution to the ancient problem. That internal rebellion, the wrenching 'no' inside Abraham's heart to the command to kill his son was what God wanted to hear. The supreme test. 'If you choose to oppose me rather than do this dreadful thing then we can *really* be friends. It's a game, don't you see! I didn't ask you to kill your son to prove your obedience to me. I asked you so that in refusing to obey me you would prove that you understood something of who I am. That I am not like the other gods. When you cry "no" to such an abomination you speak with my voice.'

Christians have not played along with God's game. We were never meant to accept the idea of Hell. We were meant to fight against it, with breaking, outraged hearts. 'Impossible! I simply refuse to accept this teaching. It's not worthy of you, Lord. It goes against everything we know of you. It's monstrous!' And then God will clap his hands with glee (are you smiling yet?): 'Bravo! If you've learned anything about me over the past six thousand years let it be this: I could never allow anyone to go to Hell.'

To believe anyone ends up in Hell (inexplicably some people actually want others to be there) is perhaps the only sin in the universe.

52   WILLIAM

It started in the usual way: the website, the chessboard of faces or torsos, the profiles underneath, aprons of titillating information. But there was something unusually striking in William's mugshot, as if caught on the wing, as if he was not really trying, as if he was busy with other things . . . as if he was somehow out of my league. His eyes were not looking into the lens of the camera but were still clear in the image, sparkling, pool-blue, a Hockney-splash into which I wanted to dive deep. Rent boys want to be rented, but William seemed unconcerned. This excited me. Then the more revealing photos were stunning. I zoomed to maximum so I could count every mole on his stomach, until his nipples were like planets filling the night sky of my computer screen.

He was hard to contact. I wrote immediately with trembling, sweaty fingers but I had to wait two weeks to get a reply. But then in his message he was friendly and fun and gave me his phone number straightaway. I left at least three voicemail messages before he got back in touch again. I was being teased and I was getting hooked. We set up a date and he gave me his address.

When I first visited his flat in Chorlton I was instantly taken aback by the soft piano music playing on a CD in his bedroom – a melancholy waltz by Chopin. Sex with prostitutes usually takes place with background music but it's either soft, soft-centred pop or a kind of flutey New Age wallpaper. Even if the guys have acid rock shattering speakers on arrival they tend to switch over to something bland and soothing before proceeding to intimacy. But never classical music. What would it be like to have sex to the rising crescendo of Rachmaninov's 2nd Symphony? A distraction actually. It is better to have the murmur of electronic vacancy which has the decency to look away from the scene of action with half-closed eyes. Rachmaninov would have shared the bed and taken up most of the space.

William's musical tastes were not sophisticated – 'Romantic Piano' was the title of this compilation – but it made him more alluring to me, as if his caresses and thrusts came from a sensitive soul. As if he meant it, I suppose I mean. Classical music looks you in the eye. It also cancels out the age gap in some way. There were around thirty years between William and myself but nearly 200 years between both of us and the Chopin waltz.

So intense was the sex we had that I returned to him again and again. And it wasn't just sex. I began to feel a sort of closeness, a desire to protect, a desire to know him more deeply. We would lie on the bed for at least ten minutes after we'd finished, talking about his family, his sister who was a nurse, his mother who, like mine, had become a widow early in life. He'd dropped out of Manchester Technical College and was basically supporting himself through prostitution, though he occasionally helped out a friend who managed a nightclub in Manchester's Gay Village. He was garrulous and happy to talk, which made it easier for me to say little. I just liked watching him, the crease in his cheek as he spoke, the lurch of his body as he stretched out lazily for a cigarette, the sweat on his chest which I had caused.

I wanted to make believe I was the only one who reclined in the curve of his naked body, but occasionally I would ask him about his life as a hustler. He always backed off: 'Oh, I never get involved. Just jerk 'em off and then take the cash. In and out. Easy money.' I was different. I had convinced myself of that. One day I bumped into one of his other customers by mistake. William had booked us too close or we had talked for too long and as I was leaving I passed a man standing downstairs at the front entrance. I saw his finger pressing the familiar buzzer. Younger than me, good-looking, tough, confident. I felt a terrible twinge of jealousy to think of him upstairs, writhing and grinding and panting and groaning on the same bed, my William's sweat all over his body. No wonder William drew back from an orgasm with me. Would the Chopin waltz be spinning once more?

William had tremendous charisma. It's hard to describe but the first time he greeted me at the door of his flat my entire being suddenly burst ablaze, flooded with radiance, like rainbow crayons colouring in the grey pencil shapes in a children's book. It wasn't so much his face, his eyes, but an overall magnetism, a pull impossible to resist. His body had the lean, muscular grace of a dancer and on the bed he moved in choreographed seduction, no second exactly the same as the last, except when he found some spot of unspeakable pleasure and repeated the detonation of its explosion in an ecstatic loop.

He could be as gentle as a breeze or he could fling me on to the mattress in a tornado of violence. One time my head smashed against the bedpost and blood flowed from a gash on my forehead down on to the pillow. Then in a shocking change of mood he became all tenderness and drew a finger of the red liquid, gently tracing patterns on my chest and on his chest like body-paint in some ancient ceremony. Time stood still as he, as if in a trance, kept circling his wet finger between our bodies until the blood had caked dry. It was weird and uncomfortable. A strange chord had been struck, out of context, in a familiar hymn tune, yet its jarring harmony seemed somehow perfect. And when the brown crust of blood liquified again later with sweat and a spurt of my semen it seemed as if I had become pagan, had gone native, was a witness to bodily fluid's irresistible reincarnation.

Sex can be repetitive, mechanical and lifeless, or it can be as varied as two faces are varied. Every movement with William was a freckle in a different place. His leg sliding against mine was never quite the same twice. The act of intercourse was always a surprise, as if he discovered a different set of nerve endings each time, as if he had a hundred different penises with which to penetrate. Even his smell changed during sex, as if the increasing heat of his body was an oven containing a casserole edged towards burning.

Nevertheless I usually left his flat with feelings of sadness. Erotic sensation had been a temporary dwelling place which, once left behind, created an intense homesickness. As I drove home the memories flashed with nostalgia, fluorescent then fading, and each stop at each traffic light (then past the shuttered supermarkets, past the endless rows of houses, past the litter-infested parks, past the empty school playgrounds) was a step down a ladder to mundanity. Pleasure's gash quickly formed a scab.

54 DISCOVERY

I always kept my priesthood and my real name secret from my hook-ups. I was usually Peter. 'A teacher and writer,' I would say when conversation arose about my job. 'Oh, I write for obscure journals about various things, theology, literature', topics I could fake if necessary. Being a writer sometimes aroused curiosity: 'Can I find your stuff online?' But mostly the interest died after I sidestepped the direct questions and as the minutes ticked away. I stayed anonymous by making the arrangements on the internet with a private email address, and if I needed to contact the guy at the last minute to change the time or check an address I kept my phone number blocked. Until William.

I'm not sure when I first suspected that drugs were part of William's life. He always had a wildness in his eyes when we had sex, a finger-to-the-wound kind of intensity. Even when we spoke afterwards, lying next to each other on the bed, legs entwined, heads close, there was a febrile energy underneath the surface. His words tumbled out just a little too quickly. His thoughts were just a little too disjointed. Then I found a syringe. I was getting dressed to leave on one occasion and my phone slipped out of my trouser pocket. As I reached for it under the bed I felt a plastic tube with a sharp point. I said nothing but I started to worry about him.

One evening after sex as we lay together he was less talkative than usual and was shaking with small convulsive twitches every few seconds. Then he began to cry. I'd never seen this side of him before and I was scared. 'Hey, William. What's the matter?' He said nothing but the convulsions became more violent and in the end the whole bed was shaking. In my desire to help him, to get closer, to share his vulnerability, and knowing at that point that he probably had a serious drug problem, I let down my guard. I held him close and began stroking his hair, then I came out with it: 'You know, there's something I haven't told you.' He looked up at me, still crying. 'In addition to teaching and writing... well,

I'm a Catholic priest.' He sniffed loudly and gradually stopped crying, his red eyes wide open with surprise.

'Wow! Why didn't you tell me?' There was a sudden change of mood, even though he was still twitching. He wiped his eyes and nose with the back of his hand. 'I've had a few priests in this bed. Where are you based?'

Instantly my pastoral instinct cooled, my safety valve re-engaged, and I knew I couldn't tell him, couldn't have him arriving at the presbytery or at Mass or at the Parish Hall. 'Oh, a church in the area,' I replied, sheepish at my own change of mood from confessional to defensive, my urge to protect him switching to an urge to protect myself.

'Yes, but where? That's really cool. I wanna come and see you at your church.' He reached over for a Kleenex to blow his nose. 'Is it a big, fancy place with lots of candles? My mum used to take me to church when I was little. I liked it at Christmas with all the lights in the dark and the crib and carols and stuff.'

Now I really regretted opening up. He continued, 'But what we did earlier. Do you not feel guilty? Isn't it, like, a sin? Can't you go to hell for that?' I looked over at the empty tube of lubricant on the bedside table and the used condom lying next to it like a squashed slug. I felt weird and uneasy and embarrassed. I was suddenly ashamed to be a priest. It seemed a stupid phantom life, like being an actor in some pathetic play for which no one had bought tickets. Reality was an erect penis entering my rectum.

'Oh well, it's just one of those things,' I said with a small, tight voice. 'As long as you love people I . . . I don't think God minds. And as long as no one is hurt.' The lameness of my response made me blush. I was shocked at the trite, imbecilic words I'd just spoken. I was sitting on a broken moral fence between the Church and the brothel and I hadn't the courage to make a decision one way or the other. He said nothing but looked unconvinced, unimpressed. Of course he did. In making such excuses I had made myself appear vastly more pathetic.

After that evening our relationship changed. He would tease me and call me Father. I hated it but obviously it amused him. 'I really wanna fuck you hard . . . *Father*. I'm feeling really horny . . . *Father*. Where's your dog-collar . . . *Father*?'

'Doesn't it bother you that I'm a priest? Don't you find it a turn-off?' I asked. I just couldn't grasp that this was all about money. Nothing I said or did or wore would increase or decrease my attractiveness to him – which was nil.

'Oh no, it's a turn-on. I think of you giving a sermon to all those old ladies and me under the pulpit giving you a blow-job, head under your robes, your cock down my throat.' It was a cruel taunting, but by that point in the evening I was already too far gone with desire to stop him. I just waited for him to run out of steam, then take off his clothes and get down to business. I just swallowed the blasphemies. I just sank deeper into the mud, under the water, no riverbank within reach.

About a month later, at the end of one of our sessions, William asked me for money beyond the usual rate. He pleaded debts, and said that he was getting tired of prostitution, that he had no other way of earning a living, that he was thinking of going back to college. I didn't mind helping him this one time so I left his flat, walked the short distance to a bank machine, then returned and pressed the familiar buzzer. How strange it was to do this in a sated state, no longer fired up with desire, no longer with finger trembling and cock stiffening. Now, in the cool of the night and the glow of the yellow street lamps, I just wanted to go home and take a shower. My hair was tousled and greasy, my body smelled of massage oil, my anus was raw and felt as if cored like an apple. I gave him three hundred pounds.

Of course, it was not the last time he asked for money.

'William, I just can't afford to keep doing this. I'm only a priest. We get a small salary and some money for weddings and funerals and so on.'

'Oh, come off it, Father. The Church is bloody loaded. Look, I'm really in a tight spot at the moment. I need some cash. Can you just go and fucking get me some money.'

His voice flashed with fury. I wasn't scared of him but I was annoyed, at his demands and at my weakness. 'OK, one last time. But you've got to get out there and find a proper job, William. You can't rely on me to keep giving you money. I just don't have it.'

'I fucking look for a fucking job every fucking…' His anger erupted but then he suddenly paused, sighed and walked over to me, slowly, heavily. 'I'm really sorry, Peter. I dunno what came over me.' He had morphed in seconds from rage to gentleness. 'But you're the only person I can ask. I really care about you and I know you want to help me get through this.' He stood close and put his arm around me, caressing my neck. 'It's tough at the moment. There are no jobs and I have bills, the rent, electricity…' He kissed my cheek as he looked at his watch, which was next to my ear. He then quickly removed his arm and walked across the room to the window, where he started to type a text on his phone. The light from its screen made an eerie shadow across his face.

'OK. Just this once, William. I'll go and get you some cash. I can only manage one hundred today though.' He finished texting and looked over at me in a slightly vacant, distracted way.

'Er…oh alright. Thanks.' His phone buzzed and he looked down again, away from me, his attention entirely consumed. I left without saying anything more and returned a few minutes later with the money. Then we parted and I walked back down the path again out to my car. As I slid my legs under the wheel and got ready to turn on the ignition to drive home I was suddenly overcome with curiosity. The texting was almost certainly an exchange with another trick arranging another encounter. As I was parked directly outside I decided to wait for a while to see what the guy looked like.

It had been a difficult day. I'd spent an hour at the hospital with a parishioner who was in a serious condition after an unsuccessful operation. I was tired. But I was curious. I would wait it out. I turned on the radio and a pert, pretty voice filled the car like a giant bouquet of flowers. I quickly turned down the volume to a level when she was just a faint aroma from the speakers. Was it Peggy Lee? The street was deserted except for a few cars which intermittently whined past.

Then after a few minutes I saw a man walking along the pavement towards my car. I hurriedly switched off the radio and sat still as he came closer and eventually arrived at the gate of William's building. I couldn't believe it! It was Father Chiwetel. He glanced at my car briefly but seemed nervous and didn't seem to notice me inside. He walked up the short path to the front door and I watched as he pressed William's buzzer, the isolated, stainless steel one underneath the others, there was no mistaking it. Then he turned around and looked back at my car which was bathed in a pool of light from the street lamp and this time our eyes met, his flashing to white, startled circles of horror in the middle of his face as he recognized me. Immediately the buzzer sounded and he disappeared inside the door like a mouse scurrying behind a skirting board. I could imagine the panic he must have been feeling. What could he do? He couldn't walk back out to the street pretending that he'd been at the wrong house. I suppose, if challenged, his defence might have been that he was visiting another flat in the building.

I'd only met him once, a few months after his arrival as a supply priest. It was at a reception after a Mass for the Family Association's annual day of recollection at the cathedral. Bishop Bernard had asked him to preach and we were all a bit surprised at this show of confidence as Chiwetel's English was fairly limited, but nevertheless the sermon proved to be impressive. He was fiery and charismatic, and he completely held our attention. I especially remember his rallying call towards the end: 'Have lots of babies! Every son or daughter is a blessing directly from God. Fill your homes with children!' This sticks in my mind because I looked around the cathedral at that point and imagined that if all the couples present were to put his exhortation into practice we would have to have mass-baptisms in nine months' time. But then he dropped a bombshell as his tone darkened. 'Let contraceptives be banished. They are rat-traps and pills of poison. More evil than abortion itself.' He paused and looked slowly around, seemingly at every individual face, inquiringly, accusingly. Even this gathering of faithful Catholics was taken aback by his directness. And now, here he was, inside William's flat, about to (it is to be hoped) roll a condom over an erect penis before engaging in acts which would fill no one's home with children.

I sat there in shock in the cold car for a minute or two and then something inside me snapped. I realized that I was not only flabbergasted at Father Chiwetel's duplicity but that I was actually jealous of, because attracted to, both of them: promiscuity's irrational code of honour, its random taboos. I looked up at the curtains. I knew the window. I could see shadows inside, the unmistakable jerking shapes of erotic encounter. I wanted desperately to be up there with both of them, one in front of me, one behind me, gorging on genitals until I choked. What a joke, with my lifeless, drained-dry dick, my varicose veins, my bunions... and twice their age? Like a spoilt child I was furious – with William, with Father Chiwetel, but most of all with myself.

I switched on the ignition and the radio and drove away, gradually calming down in my state of utter exhaustion. The cheery music (from the same singer as before) was a distraction and I was looking forward to taking a long, hot shower at home. Then, strangely, I began to feel pity for Chiwetel, conscious of the turmoil which must have been raging inside him and aware that those who fulminate most vehemently against sins of the flesh are often those most likely to be indulging in them. Being discovered visiting a male prostitute would almost certainly have meant him being sent back to Nigeria where he could have faced prison or worse. A significant financial commitment must have been made to enable him to move to England in the first place and I'm sure he was the pride of his community back home. Now I started to worry about him. I wondered if I should phone the next day and reassure him that I wouldn't tell anyone. But that would mean revealing my own relationship with William, which I wasn't prepared to do. As it stood he could always claim that it was another man standing in the porch that evening, and I could always claim that I was visiting someone else in the neighbourhood – my word against his word. Best to leave it.

The song finished. The announcer's voice. It *was* Peggy Lee.

56   BLACKMAIL

I didn't contact William for a couple of weeks after that evening but then one afternoon the presbytery landline phone rang. It was him. I felt a chill.

'How did you get this number, William?'

'Google. I just went through every priest in the area and checked out photos. It was easy. Why haven't you phoned? I miss you, Peter . . . er, Father. When are you coming over again? I'm feeling really horny right now. You make me so hard. I want you to suck my big dick.' I was scared. Now he knew where I lived. Now I had lost control of the situation which I had so carefully managed with private emails and blocked phone numbers. I got in touch with him when I wanted to see him. I drove over. I took off my clothes. We had sex. I paid him. I left and drove home. But now he was in the driving seat.

'William, I've decided that I'm not going to see you anymore. Please don't call me again or get in touch.' I was shaking as I put down the phone.

I heard nothing from him for a few days but I was in a constant state of dread in case he knocked on my door or even appeared at Mass, sitting in the congregation, smirking, leering, coming up for Communion, confronting me afterwards at the back of the church. Every time I left the presbytery I feared seeing him outside on the street. I didn't fear him physically but I was terrified at the thought of the embarrassment he could cause me.

Then one afternoon the phone rang again.

'Hi Father, how are you? Hey, I'm ... I'm really in a bad way. I need some money. I could always come over to your place.'

I sat at my desk, weighing up the situation. There was no way I was going to invite him to the presbytery, but what could he really do to harm me? He could be a nuisance but there was no evidence that we had even met, and priests meet all sorts of strange characters in the course of their ministry. No one had seen me at his flat, except that one client who was arriving early as I was leaving late, and Father Chiwetel of course. There was no proof. I decided to tough it out.

'Listen William, it is *over* between us. I want you to stop phoning me. I'm not going to give you any more money and I don't want to see you for sex again. It's finished. I really wish you well but you must stop getting in touch. OK ... bye.' I put down the phone and felt a relief. Five minutes later it rang again.

'Father Joseph?' The voice was cheerful and confident.

'William, I thought I told ... '

'There's something I want you to hear, Father.'

'I'm not interested, William. I'm going to put down the phone now. Please stop bothering ... '

'Father, I think you . . . might want to hear this.' There was a brief pause, a soft click, and then I listened in absolute horror. I heard my voice, and my groans: 'Fuck me, fuck me, oh yeah, oh fuck, oh that feels so good.' The puerile chant of primeval lust. It was definitely my voice. How on earth had he recorded us having sex? The sound faded as he lifted the phone back up to his ear but I could still hear the inane words continuing in the distance.

'Sounds good, doesn't it! You were really into it. My hot fucking priest. Do you know what's *really* cool?' He paused, then laughed. 'That's just the soundtrack. There are images too. I filmed us a few times on my laptop. You know how it was always open on my desk? Well, the camera was pointing at the bed and I got some really good footage of you. Really close shots! "Fuck me, fuck me" with your face in full view.' He laughed loudly and in the background I could hear more sounds of me shouting, 'Oh yeah, oh yeah.'

Now I was completely mortified, and really scared. He didn't have to make explicit the potential for damage that this recording had.

'So,' all amusement was now absent from his hardened voice, 'I want cash, Father. Like tonight.'

It didn't take me long in my state of panic to respond. 'I'll come over later this evening. What time are you free?' My voice was dull and expressionless.

'Anytime after nine is good . . . three hundred pounds, OK?'

'I'll see you later, William.'

I felt as if my whole life had melted in front of me, like I was a snowman watching himself being reduced to a pool of water, seeping away into the muddy undergrowth. I was angry at him and at myself. The potential for blackmail from this was limitless; it would be my perpetual shadow. I knew I couldn't keep the cash flowing but I needed to buy some time.

Later that evening I arrived at his flat, he buzzed me in, and I walked slowly up the staircase. There he was at the front door, smiling, wild-eyed, flushed. I handed over the money and turned away to leave but he said, 'Father, do you not want to see the film? It's really cool.' I wanted this film to be swallowed up in a black hole somewhere, and the thought of watching it, especially with him next to me, was repulsive beyond words. But there was a scintilla of curiosity, and moreover a desire to know just how incriminating it was. Could the images be mistaken for someone else? Perhaps it was blurred and patchy? I looked at him long and cold and then stepped silently inside the door, closing it behind me. We walked into the bedroom; his laptop was already open.

The picture was amazingly clear, and at first I just watched, numb and speechless. But then, such is the unpredictable lunacy of human beings, I began to feel vanity, a regret at how unattractive I looked on the screen. My fat, white legs spread, feet twisted and calloused, everything loose and frumpy and flabby and . . . old. Did I *really* look that old? The footage only showed flashes of his back but the contrast was cruel. His athletic torso, with its tattoo between arched shoulder blades, lean, taut and glistening with sweat, was thrusting itself against me with tremendous energy, whilst my face, blotchy and greasy with its soft mouth, was spouting the idiotic words of rough sex I'd learned from watching porno videos. I thought this pathetic lingo would turn him on, that it was expected of me. And every time I said 'Fuck, yeah' and he replied with 'Fuck, yeah', a tennis match was in progress, verbal balls across the net in a game which would have been risible but for the power of the brain's dopamine fix. I turned away burning with shame and walked out of the flat without saying a word.

His demands for money continued. 'Can't you take something from the collection plate, Father?' Good suggestion. It was all I could do as my savings account was getting low. No holiday this year. Then eventually I realized that things could not continue like this. I was exhausted through lack of sleep and was feeling completely desperate. I decided with a kind of reckless courage to phone Bishop Bernard's office and request an urgent meeting with him. He had had a cancellation the following week and so I went to see him. I started by explaining that I was being blackmailed and that the instigator had material which was genuine and which was grossly incriminating and... then I just told him the whole story. I was in such a state of despair that I didn't care anymore. He listened quietly, attentively, and when I had finished he completely took my breath away.

'Father Joseph, this is a terrible situation. You don't need me to tell you that. But before we talk any more about it…'
He came around from behind his desk and sat next to me in a vacant chair. He spoke slowly, thoughtfully: 'I know this is going to seem completely mad in your present state of distress, but I think this is a special moment of grace for you. You have reached the very bottom of the pit. There's nowhere to escape. You're totally trapped. And Christ, who faced suffering and disgrace and death, is waiting there for you. "Neither do I condemn you," he said to the woman who had been caught in the act of adultery. Her situation was pretty similar to yours if you think about it. You've been caught in the act, on film even, and our Lord is offering you his hand of support and friendship and forgiveness. He is with you. And I am with you as your bishop, every step of the way. He will not abandon you and neither will I.'

He stood up and walked back behind his desk. 'I don't know how we're going to handle this, Father, but…' He paused, looking down at his hands, then he looked up at me: 'Father, I want you to go on a retreat. An eight-day silent retreat at Craigbourne. There's one starting this coming Monday and I want you to go. I'll sort out a replacement priest for your parish. I know it seems impossible but just try to forget this whole business for the week. Push it to the back of your mind. Then come and see me when you get home again. There's been nothing criminal here, no one raped or underage, and the money you took from the collection we'll treat as borrowing and I'll pay it back from my own bank account. Breathe freely in the presence of God whose compassion is infinite and unconditional.'

I couldn't speak as the tears were welling up in my eyes and my throat was tight. Of course I had to go on the retreat. I went home to make some practical preparations and although I would have liked more time to think things through I could see that it was better to do it immediately. The following evening the phone rang and it was William again. I felt much less dread now and I told him quietly, kindly, that these phone calls had to stop.

'It's no use threatening me now, William. I've been to see my bishop and he knows everything. I will not give you any more money and I suggest you delete that film and that we just forget this whole business.' I put down the phone with a light heart.

57 OINTMENT

'Today I want you to focus on repentance, on the transforming love which changes a cold, hardened sinner into a man on fire for God and souls.' The week is drawing to a close. I've become used to Father Neville's visits. I'm no longer repelled by his priggishness. His platitudes pass me by. 'The woman with the alabaster jar, from St Luke's Gospel. A sinner who, in an act of contrite devotion, anoints the feet of the Holy One with expensive ointment, filling the house with its perfume. This is our vocation as priests: to turn from sin, to give everything to God, then to spread the fragrance of His love to those in our care. Read the story over many times, Father, and let it speak to you, inspire you.' He got up to leave. There had hardly been a moment for me to say anything, if I'd had anything to say. I think by this point he's given up on me.

After a few mind-wandering minutes I opened my Bible to Luke. I'd read this passage hundreds of times but I settled down to do so again with just a little more concentration than usual. Yes, this intriguing woman, known in the village as a sinner. Who was she? She is shown here as a prostitute but one who kisses the feet of Jesus, her hair tumbling all over them. At that time and in that place, when women routinely kept their heads covered, this was almost the equivalent of going topless. Then there's more. She pours luxurious lotion on to his feet, wiping off the sticky oil with her hair, a dribbling mess everywhere. Did Luke fully grasp the scene he was creating, its sensual charge, its scandalous implications? The disciples object, but at the waste of money, not at the impropriety. Christ and the reflexologist. Were his feet sensitive like mine? Did he give in to a shiver of delight as his toes were tickled?

The story appears almost identically in the gospels of Matthew and Mark. I read through each of these, trying to recreate the scene in my mind, trying to put myself in the place of this woman. But then in John's Gospel something new. The story is similar but now the woman is identified as Mary from Bethany, sister of Martha and Lazarus, and no longer a prostitute but a close friend of Jesus. Could it really be the same woman, the same story? And now only one of the disciples is objecting – Judas Iscariot. 'Why was this ointment not sold for three hundred *denarii* and given to the poor?' he asks. John comments that Judas didn't care about the poor but instead would line his own pockets from the common purse. But perhaps he did care for the poor. Perhaps John just didn't realize where the money was going and was making an unfair presumption. 'Let not your left hand know what your right hand is doing,' said Christ. In a heart troubled with doubts and shattered dreams perhaps trying to alleviate the suffering of the destitute was all Judas had left. 'Sell all you own, give to the poor, and follow me,' Christ had taught them. Why was he now permitting this woman to be so wasteful? Why was he allowing such extravagance, such an ego trip? Judas' resentment increased. He felt outside the group, these uneducated oafs, these religious nutters, these gullible sycophants. But what hurt him most was that Jesus, whom he loved, seemed to be so much more affectionate to them than to him. After this episode with the profligate woman and her perfume perhaps now was the time for Judas to leave the group. Or to force Jesus' hand...

58 ISCARIOT

'So how much is it worth to you?' Judas asks. 'I should be able to catch him in an unguarded moment. Fifty silver pieces?' The priests mutter amongst themselves and finally bargain Judas down to thirty and he goes off shining with energy, jangling the coins in his pocket, waiting for the right moment.

'Is it I . . . is it I?' The disciples at the supper table ask like silly children who the betrayer will be, as if Fate had already made the decision. Jesus dips a piece of bread into the sauce and hands it, dripping, to Judas. 'What you're going to do, do quickly.'

Oh? Not a plea to change my mind? I might be wavering, Lord. A doubt is hovering around me like a bird about to perch on a branch. I thought you might say to me, 'Judas, you don't need to do this. We can still be friends. I know the mistakes you've made, but they are forgiven, forgotten.' But no, you tell me to go ahead and do it. Quickly even.

Judas scrambles away from the table, still munching on the morsel, hiding tears of shame and anger. Loneliness overwhelms him, a loneliness which doesn't depend on the presence or absence of companions. Com-pan-ions: the dipped bread from supper which he has just swallowed leaves a bitter taste in his mouth.

'This way. I know where he will be.' Judas is leading the soldiers along. The clank of weapons. The ribald jokes. The cold night. They arrive at the garden and Judas approaches Jesus, trying to avoid his eyes. Closer. Moving rightwards, pretending to look into the distance, and then an awkward, hasty turn to the left to place his pursed lips against the prickle of beard.

'My friend, do what you are here for,' Jesus says in a quiet voice, heavy but kind.

Judas wants to ask, 'Is it too late to embrace you, never to depart from you again? I remember our joyous times together, the long carefree journeys, the discomforts which never seemed to matter.' But the soldiers are close behind, impatient, breath steaming into the night, tipsy from cheap wine. Everything is set on its course.

'Whom do you seek?' asks Jesus in a firmer, louder voice, looking past Judas. Why is he so calm, so regal, so commanding? He seems to combine the authority of Caesar with the disarming simplicity of a child. The soldiers stammer, suddenly drained of courage: 'Jesus of Nazareth.' They feel inexplicably out of their depth, foolish, fearful, confused.

'I am he,' is his reply, words as powerful, as elemental as 'Let there be light.' The soldiers crumple to the ground and Judas is suddenly terrified. This has all gone horribly wrong. It has moved from the domestic to the universal and there is no going back. His heart breaks open with despair and self-loathing, a dry vessel which crumbled easily.

The soldiers scramble to their feet again, angry at having shown weakness, impatient now to finish the business at hand and get back indoors to the warmth and the wine. They grab hold of Jesus, pushing aside Judas who stumbles then sprints away from Gethsemane, straight to the chief priests and elders.

'I have betrayed innocent blood' he cries as he bursts through the door, reaching into his pocket to pull out the shoal of silver coins and flinging them across the room. They ricochet on the stone-cold floor, their flickering flight coming to rest in every corner: pearls before swine, stars in a bleak, blank sky.

'What is that to us?' the priests say. A door is closed by man as well as by God. Judas leaves and loiters along the hidden streets until the fresh light of dawn begins to clarify everything except the turmoil in his heart.

Done. I have betrayed innocent blood but I have returned the blood money. What now? As the day brightens his mind snaps back into focus and he starts feverishly on the road to Calvary. He is late. Time hurtles forward as the memories flood back. He is in the middle of the moment which will divide the centuries: BC/AD, the crossroads, the fault line, the meridian of history. He has seized destiny by the throat and his whole being suddenly wants to sing for joy. And maybe he can still stop the murder itself. He continues to race, lungs surging, blood pumping: 'Perhaps it's not too late.' Stones fly sharply to the side of the road in his haste. Hope erupts inside him, an ocean of hope thrashing him from side to side in its surf.

The memories. The miracles. That woman bent double who stood up erect. Bartimeus' yelp of joy when he could see for the first time. The five thousand fed. The leper's pustules blanched to smooth skin. And the voice into the face of that terrible storm, boat lurching, water swamping, everyone seasick: 'Be still.' And it was still. The deepest calm. The moon a circular slick of off-white paint floating on the flat, black lake. He had smiled at Judas that time.

He's still running, breathless, dry-throated . . . but then different memories return. Older ones. The good times before he met Christ. The profitable marketplace. The rich, spicy food. The sophistication of his friends with their easy banter into the night. His flirtatious words and the women's subsequent slither of assent as they accompanied him coyly into the shadows, his hands fumbling through garments to the hot breasts underneath.

His mood shifts. He's panting. A wince of pain in his winded chest. His steps slow. His thumping heart gradually settles back to its normal rate. His blood becomes heavier in his veins. Then he stops. Ruddy. Sweaty. He can't continue. His hopes are a game. Mind's hopscotch. Holiday's holiday from homework. The Christ episode these past three years . . . an impetuous fantasy which already seems like it happened to someone else.

He crouches down at the side of the road to rest and think for a while. Lack of sleep and purpose curdle his former zeal. He looks down at the sandy ground, his mind a blank, his eyes unfocused. He begins to trace abstract patterns in the dust with a finger, grit gathering under his nails. Finally he stands up again, wearily, hopelessly, with an emptiness deeper than the core of the earth and a desolation he can taste like heartburn. He turns around and retraces his steps, now walking soberly, bashful as he notices along the way the smudged tracks of his earlier jejune enthusiasm. He feels like he has aged ten years in the last ten minutes. He puts his hands in his pockets...what's this? A coin. He takes it out and it glints in the sun. He must have flung only twenty-nine at the feet of the priests. One silver piece. Enough for some good meals, some good fucks, maybe even a new life away from all this religious insanity.

'Consider the birds of the air' – around him wheel vultures, sharp-beaked, merciless.

'Your Heavenly Father feeds them' – what, on carcasses pecked through to the intestine?

'Consider the lilies of the field' – around him mere tufts of scrub, dust-dry thistles poking out of the pale ground as if randomly stuck there rather than rooted.

He continues walking alone along the road, until he finally finds himself at Hakeldama and the safety of its caves. As he approaches he notices a tree, gnarled and hideous, next to one of the barren rocks. He feels for the rope around his waist. It is too late. The wedding banquet has begun, the Bridegroom has gone inside and the door has been locked. He is not on the guest list. He walks towards the tree.

'Father forgive me for I know what I am doing.' A tiny brown bird alights on one of the branches, perches for a few seconds, looks around brightly, then flies carelessly away.

'My God, my God, why have I forsaken thee?' He is disconsolate, empty. 'What you're going to do, do quickly.' Jesus' words to him last night. Would he say it to him now?

He stands under the tree and flings off his fear like a cloak.

He unties the rope from around his waist and quickly climbs the four or five ledges of the rock face, dislodging weeds and loose soil. Looping the rope around the strongest branch he ties a firm knot and from there puts his neck through the noose.

It is finished. Life has a limited span and sometimes it needs to be made just that bit shorter by our own hand. He tries to recall some comforting words of Jesus before his slump to oblivion. Nothing comes to mind except that cold, dismissive phrase: 'What you're going to do, do quickly.'

But then words fade and a nebulous image begins to form in his mind. Eyes. Those eyes he had avoided catching when kissing Jesus in betrayal now return in memory. Judas suddenly finds his own eyes moist, brimming with tears – not of remorse or repentance, nor of hope, but of . . . mirth! In a flash he realizes that even now this need not be the end. Nothing is lost. The door is not closed or locked after all. There is no guest list. The bridesmaids are all brides, eagerly sought by their Bridegroom. The hungry one to be fed is Judas!

Astonishment overwhelms him and he grasps the coarse rope, fumbling frantically with the knot he had tied so tightly, but before he can loosen it . . . CRACK. A massive earthquake shakes the ground. It is the ninth hour. Over in Jerusalem the curtain in the Temple is being torn from top to bottom and there is suddenly a terrible darkness over the land. The gnarled tree splits in two and Judas lurches forward, falling on his stomach on to one of the sharper edges of the rock. The rope is stretched to choking-point and Judas gasps for breath. Soon ants begin to swarm through the gaping hole where his guts are spilling out into the sombre afternoon.

A few miles away another stomach has been torn open, pierced by a lance as it hangs on a cross, and eleven men are running away in fear and cowardice. But here, smashed on a rock, supper for insects, gagging for oxygen, a man is resplendent with joy, with unspeakable love. Judas looks into two eyes:

'Today thou shalt be with me in Paradise.'

59   FINAL MORNING

I'm sitting in the chapel. Alone. Packed. Breakfasted. The eight days are over. I look over at the altar with glazed eyes, as unseeing as two lychees. I'm tired. Sadness sits just under my ribcage, at rest but still on its haunches.

My mind turns to my parishioners. They put their trust in me, but I have abused that trust. My heart tears apart as I think of this, as if I had been asked to guard a baby in a pram outside a shop but had walked away, leaving it unattended.

I think everyone else has left now. Cars have been firing up and bumping away down the muddy path for the past hour, one after another. Outside the window I hear the continuing rain and inside a vacuum cleaner is whining in the corridor in preparation for the next guests. It's time to go. I'm putting the cap on my pen.

It's now a couple of weeks since the retreat. Leaving Craigbourne and driving home in the rain I felt fragile but healing. The wound was still there but so were the stitches, and something (someone?) was giving me confidence to take the small steps ahead, despite everything that awaited me.

But as I arrived home, parked the car, opened the boot, lifted out and carried my bags to the house, turned the key in the front door, pushed it open, pulled out the key, laid down my bags by the stairs, closed the door, took off my wet anorak, hung it loosely by its hood on the banister, then walked into my cold, damp study with its foggy memories of mediocrity and worse, there was a disconnect. It felt like I had woken up after a heavy slumber – an unrefreshing nap wasting the best part of the day. The dream of recovery had vanished. The small consolations which I had collected in the latter part of the retreat had now evaporated. The Gospels were dead letters to me once more – just blank sheets of paper. Only that one-sentence note of encouragement from Bishop Bernard remained as a watermark under the surface. An espresso shot for sure, but ultimately an ephemeral stimulation on which it was not possible to build an entire spiritual life. I am a priest. I am meant to have resources of spiritual strength for others. Sitting down at my desk again next to a pile of unopened post in the darkening afternoon I realized that my fuel tank was empty. Only dregs remained. The engine was dead.

But I was reluctant to admit this and with a reflex of conformity and mendacity I started to write a letter to the bishop. Pen on paper, phrases flowing... 'the courage to make a new start'... 'the resolve to try again'... 'leaving everything in the hands of God'... 'a new humility'... but it was all so hollow. Someone else was writing the words with my hand. I scrunched the paper into a tight ball and dropped it into the wastepaper basket. I looked around my study with all of its mess, the children's liturgy handbooks, the Bibles, the bills, the junk. The sheer ugliness and dreariness of my life. Turning on my computer I logged on to check my emails – 78 messages. I scrolled down the list and there was one from William. He'd never sent me an email before, only phone calls and texts, but now he knew where I lived he'd obviously been able to find the address on the parish website. His message had a paperclip symbol next to the 'subject' heading. My lethargic melancholy flashed to panic and I felt a prickling across my head. I knew what it contained and although I was not going to open the attachment I did click on the email itself to see if there was an accompanying text.

'Hi Father, what's up? Movie time :-)'

I should just have ignored it, deleted it, carried on sorting out my inbox, but I felt the strangest cocktail of emotions: fear – the blackmail had begun again; zeal – to be for William what the bishop had been for me; and lust – a flush around my loins. My body was a triptych of contradictions: head sweating with panic, heart dilating with compassion, groin throbbing with desire. I dialled his number.

'William, I just got your email. I . . .'

'Hey Father' he interrupted, affably. 'Haven't heard from you for a while! Why don't you come over? I'd really like to see you.'

My hands trembled and my resolve began to crumble. I wanted to run away, but also I wanted to help him. I could see the path ahead and it was not just dangerous but hopeless. I knew he was a mess, no money, no job, on drugs. But then with an insane illogic I convinced myself that I could be a pastor for him, as if I were some heroic, self-sacrificing priest like the Curé of Ars. After all, I have the same grace of state as the saints. God would surely protect me and enable me to bring comfort to this troubled soul. And what a supreme act of forgiveness it would be for me to help William, despite him causing me such distress.

I shut my brain down and began to think only with my heart, to embrace the danger as if on a battlefield carrying the Sacrament to a dying soldier. I began to feel an awakening of evangelical fervour, as if after twenty-five soporific years of mediocrity my vocation might finally have found its meaning. I thought of those holy pictures in my mother's missal, of missionary priests lifting up crucifixes in alien lands, trekking through dense jungles to hear Confessions, saying Masses in tin shacks in remote villages, founding orphanages for abandoned children and hospitals for the dying. Suddenly I had a sense of the logic and beauty of traditional piety and of Catholicism's clean, clear, neatly ordered doctrinal system. I imagined myself back in the library at Craigbourne but this time taking Tanquerey's *The Spiritual Life* back to my room and delving into it, studying it, underscoring the more challenging passages, carrying a battered copy under the arm of my cassock.

'I'll be over as soon as I can.' I grabbed my wet anorak and got back into my car, leaving behind the emails, the problems of the other souls in my care, the handing-over from my supply priest, the note unwritten to my bishop, my bags still unpacked in the hallway. I was fired up by the thought that I could rescue William. Of course I realize today that I am the last person who could have done this. I didn't grasp that he was not going to see me in a new light after only nine days. The retreat had seemed to me like a whole chapter of my life; for him it was just an unread page, an incomprehensible irrelevance. Driving along the familiar roads I might as well have been on horseback in a Hollywood movie. I couldn't see it clearly at the time but my awakened missionary spirit was a temporary, immature, emotional reflex. And it was shot through with vanity. This was all about *me* playing the romantic lead. It was all about *my* sentimentality, *my* self-justification, *my* heroism.

I parked outside his house and walked up to the front door. As I pressed the cold, stainless-steel buzzer I was suddenly overwhelmed with memories and my resolve began to weaken. I was tempted to walk away, drive home, without a word. I should have done so. It would have been kinder to him and to me. Too late.

The front door sprung open and I walked up the staircase, its familiarity both sickening and comforting. It felt like I'd been there the day before but also like it had been years since my last visit. I reached his flat and the door was ajar – I could see he was standing inside. I paused for a second, then stepped into the space where I'd spent so many hours . . . of sex, only sex. The flare of excitement before and during; the sad subsidence afterwards. Condom packets torn open, sperm shooting, then Kleenex boxes emptied, grubby twenty-pound notes counted out, the shameful slinking away. The lie of our physical passion: closer than close in the sticky embrace and in the one-flesh of penetration, then distant and cold as a star in the slow aftermath.

We stood by his dining table with the grease-stained pizza box and the empty beer cans. Unlike before I was not here to have sex and I realized that I had nothing to say to him, that I really didn't care about him at all. My pastoral impulses were fast fading. The holy pictures had slipped out of the missal.

'I've missed you,' he said, smiling. His insincerity riled me even if his smile charmed a little. He was still hot, sexy. He walked over and put his arm around me, giving me a kiss on the cheek and caressing my neck. We said nothing. I wanted to speak, to say the words of priestly consolation which had flowed so easily in the car, but now they had dried up. He kept caressing my neck, moving across to my shoulders in a gentle massage.

'Feel good?' He undid a couple of buttons on my shirt. I stopped him abruptly.

'William! I want to talk to you.' His eyes flashed with surprise and he stood back. I fastened the two buttons of my shirt and started to speak, more formally, stiffly than I intended. 'I've been on retreat and things have changed in my life. I'm not going to be seeing you or any other prostitutes again. I've been stupid and I'm determined to change, to turn over a new leaf. I told you I'm not going to give you any more money and I've driven over here to...' I hesitated as I couldn't think of the right words to describe why I was standing there in the first place. I could have said all of this in a phone call or even an email. I started up again. 'I'm determined to make a clean break. I wish you well, William, but I don't want to see you anymore. You need to go to rehab and sort out your drug problem and get yourself a proper job. Prostitution is never a good way to live. Your shelf life is limited and then what will you do?' I was on a roll now, a smug, garrulous roll. I felt like I had escaped through a trap door and was turning the energy of my relief into pompous verbosity. 'I suggest you delete that film and we'll forget any of this ever happened. You do realize that you were blackmailing me, which is a criminal offence – I have evidence. I've spoken to my bishop and told him everything and he's completely supportive of me. It's so nice when the boss understands,' I crowed, with a soft chuckle.

Thinking back to this just two weeks later I can't believe I said such stupid, trite things. I could see him getting angry, his body tensing like that of an animal in danger, but I felt like

I was safe, as if standing next to a locked cage at the zoo. I was almost taunting him in my new flush of confidence. I'd written him off. He was history. I'd caught the train and I could see him, standing on the platform, left behind. My *schadenfreude* was fairly innocuous though: I dearly hoped he would catch the next train but I was just terribly pleased that I would get there first.

'You fuck.' He spoke quietly, almost in a whisper. I looked into his face and it was contorted with hatred. I'd never seen an expression like this, on him or anyone else. I smiled and was about to say something else lighthearted and jocular to defuse the situation.

'You FUCK!' he shouted now and stepped closer to me. 'You miserable, pompous shit. How can you stand there like some fucking schoolteacher.' He paused and looked me up and down with contempt. 'And "shelf life"? You were never on the shelf, you ugly fucker. You think I fancy you coz we screw around. You make me sick. You're ugly and boring. I hate it after sex when you wanna talk and be all romantic and shit, arm around me, hands through my hair. Makes me wanna fucking throw up. I was thinking money every bloody second. And now you tell me to get a job and sort myself out and stop scoring tricks. Go to hell!'

I was red with embarrassment. I began to realize how sanctimonious and insensitive I must have sounded. I looked around his bedsit again and realized how hard it would be for him to change, to leave this wretched life. He came over to me and put his arm around my neck, but tightly this time.

'Fucker,' he said quietly, looking into my eyes. I couldn't hold his stare and began to tremble. Now I was really scared. I thought he was going to punch me. His face was almost touching mine and I could smell his breath, see the malice in his wild eyes, feel his body tense next to mine. Then his body was actually against mine, front to front. He hugged me tight, teeth bared, and began to grind against me. It was a simulated sex act but violent and cold. He was strong and I had no chance against him. Continuing this strange dance of gyration he moved me towards the bed and flung me down on the mattress. I was terrified and completely unaroused. Every other time I'd been on this bed there had been piano music playing on his CD player but now all I could hear was the occasional car or squeal of children playing in the street outside. He started to undress me and I tried to resist, tried to push his arm to one side, to kick him off me, but it was no good. I gave up the struggle, thought it was safer. I lay limp on the bed whilst he pulled down my trousers and underpants. He then grabbed a remote control, pointed it at the television and pushed a button. A porno video started on the screen, two impossibly beautiful young men having sex by a swimming pool in glamorous grounds on a sunny day, most likely somewhere in Southern California. He looked intensely at the images for a while, holding me down, then he unbuttoned his jeans and began stimulating himself to an erection.

No condom, no lubrication, no words. After ten minutes of pain and humiliation to the utmost degree, his eyes on the television screen the whole time, he had his orgasm, inside me. I had become numb and vacant on every level, as if I'd just jumped off a high building into an abyss. I'd been raped. What next? He cleaned himself up, buttoned up his jeans, stood up and lit a cigarette.

'Does that feel better, Father? You didn't get a hard-on today though. Tired after your retreat?' He clicked the video off and picked up his phone to check for messages. The room was dark and silent. My heart was as if skinned alive. We had both wallowed in self-loathing. There was nothing to say. I left the flat and drove home in pain. Utterly empty.

I'm so scared. Of so many things. I'm constantly panicky. I just can't function as a priest anymore. I can't bear to talk to people in the parish. I don't want to eat. I can't read. I sit in front of the television without watching it. I go to bed early, tired but unable to sleep. I wander around in a daze. I've lost all interest in sex. I'm scared of my future but scared that I don't even want a future. I just can't imagine how it's possible to continue like this. And I'm frightened of William. He's sent me three texts since the rape mentioning again the film of us having sex. He can send it to anyone, anytime, with one click of his mouse.

Then this morning he showed up at Mass, the only person in the small congregation who was under sixty and not female, and sat at the back playing around with his phone. At the end of the Mass after everyone had left he remained in his pew and I went over to where he was slumped. I warned him again that the bishop knew everything and that I had evidence of criminal blackmail. Yet how could I ever face taking him to court? The jury watching my leering, lascivious face on the video.

I suppose the only cure now would be some kind of spiritual radiation but my tumour is too far gone and I'd rather just let nature take its course. I could never be a St Alphonsus. Mortification would be to me an extension of my self-hatred. I couldn't take it seriously. The breakdown of my cells is inevitable. A creeping decay . . . until nothing is left.

EPILOGUE

FROM: Rev. Luke Tremont
TO: Bishop Bernard Smith
SUBJECT:
DATE: 1 December 2010   8:04 AM

MEMORIAL OF BLESSED CHARLES DE FOUCAULD

Your Grace,

I've just got off the phone with the house-keeper of Sacred Heart parish in Sale. She discovered the dead body of Fr Joseph Flynn this morning in his study. It looks like it was suicide as there were knife wounds to his wrists. I've notified the police and I'm about to drive over there to see if there's anything I can do. I'll phone you later.

In Christ,

Fr Luke
Secretary to the Bishop of Altrincham

My dearest Chiwetel,

I've been trying to phone you for the past two days. Is everything OK?

This business with Fr Joseph is so upsetting. The police came to see me this morning as it seems there's some doubt as to whether he actually killed himself. It looks like there were suspicious circumstances – a head wound in addition to the slashed wrists. They wanted to ask me some questions and they left me some notebooks they found in his desk at the time of his death which they've asked me to read. I just can't bear to do this at the moment.

I need to see you. I just want you to hold me in your arms tonight. How blessed we are to have each other! Can you come over later? Send me an email or phone me.

Love you!

Bernard ×

The Final Retreat
© STEPHEN HOUGH, 2018

Stephen Hough is a concert pianist,
a composer and a writer. Named by *The
Economist* as one of 20 Living Polymaths, he
was the first classical performer to be awarded
a MacArthur Fellowship and was made a
Commander of the Order of the British
Empire in 2014. He has been published
by *The Times, The Guardian* and
The Daily Telegraph.

Design: ORNAN ROTEM
Set in Monotype Bulmer
Cover: NUM STIBBE

Image on previous page:
Anton Kolig, *Seated Youth*, 1919 ©DACS 2017
©Leopold Museum, Wien/Manfred
Thumberger · Reproduced with permission

Printed and bound in Germany by
Optimal Media on Fedrigoni's Corolla Book

ISBN: 978-1-909631-28-1

SYLPH EDITIONS

LONDON · 2018
www.sylpheditions.com